## "There's no way i

Emily stared at him with fury in her eyes. It was incredible that he was saying this to her now. Ten years too late! "Get this straight, Cooper Dunn, I am no concern of yours. You might own part of this ranch, but you don't own me."

Emily took a deep breath to get her anger under control. "My being pregnant has nothing to do with you," she told him.

"But you need someone here to look after you."

The gentle regard on his face both touched and infuriated her. If only he'd shown her as much ten years ago.

"You're not a man who could stay in one place for more than a week, much less look after a pregnant woman."

But, oh, how her heart wished he was that man!

Dear Reader,

*Unforgettable Bride,* by bestselling author Annette Broadrick, is May's VIRGIN BRIDES selection, *and* the much-requested spin-off to her DAUGHTERS OF TEXAS series. Rough, gruff rodeo star Bobby Metcalf agreed to a quickie marriage—sans honeymoon!—with virginal Casey Carmichael. But four years later, he's still a married man—one intent on being a husband to Casey in every sense....

Fabulous author Arlene James offers the month's FABULOUS FATHERS title, *Falling for a Father of Four.* Orren Ellis was a single dad to a brood of four, so hiring sweet Mattie Kincaid seemed the perfect solution. Until he found himself falling for this woman he could never have.... Stella Bagwell introduces the next generation of her bestselling TWINS ON THE DOORSTEP series. In *The Rancher's Blessed Event,* an ornery bronc rider must open his heart both to the woman who'd betrayed him...and her child yet to be born.

Who can resist a sexy, stubborn cowboy—particularly when he's your husband? Well, Taylor Cassidy tries in Anne Ha's *Long, Tall Temporary Husband.* But will she succeed? And Sharon De Vita's irresistible trio, LULLABIES AND LOVE, continues with *Baby with a Badge,* where a bachelor cop finds a baby in his patrol car...and himself in desperate need of a woman's touch! Finally, new author C.J. Hill makes her commanding debut with a title that sums it up best: *Baby Dreams and Wedding Schemes.*

Romance has everything you need from new beginnings to tried-and-true favorites. Enjoy each and every novel this month, and every month!

Warm Regards!

*Joan Marlow Golan*

Joan Marlow Golan
Senior Editor, Silhouette Romance

Please address questions and book requests to:
Silhouette Reader Service
U.S.: 3010 Walden Ave., P.O. Box 1325, Buffalo, NY 14269
Canadian: P.O. Box 609, Fort Erie, Ont. L2A 5X3

# STELLA Bagwell

# THE RANCHER'S BLESSED EVENT

Silhouette
ROMANCE™
Published by Silhouette Books
America's Publisher of Contemporary Romance

To Mary-Theresa Hussey and Melissa Senate.

Thanks for keeping the Murdock family alive!

 SILHOUETTE BOOKS

ISBN 0-373-19296-7

THE RANCHER'S BLESSED EVENT

**Printed in U.S.A.**

**Books by Stella Bagwell**

## *STELLA BAGWELL*

sold her first book to Silhouette in November 1985. Now, more than thirty novels later, she is still thrilled to see her books in print and can't imagine having any other job than that of writing about two people falling in love.

She lives in a small town in southeastern Oklahoma with her husband of twenty-six years. She has one son and daughter-in-law.

Dear Reader,

Writing a trilogy is a lot like reading one. In the process you become so attached to the same characters, you grow very reluctant to finally tell them goodbye. Such was the case when I finished the last of my TWINS ON THE DOORSTEP trilogy. So you can imagine what a special thrill it was for me when my editor asked if I would like to continue writing about the Murdock family!

Telling you how Rose, Justine and Chloe found their twin siblings—and love in the bargain—was pure pleasure for me. And I would like to express a big thank-you to all you readers who read and responded so warmly to each book. You are the reason my job is so rewarding, and I can't convey how much I appreciate each and every one of you.

Now with great delight, I would like to invite you back to Lincoln County, New Mexico, where you'll find old familiar friends and meet new ones, too. Beginning with Emily Hamilton and her unexpected reunion with an old flame, you'll find the Murdock children have all grown up and, ready or not, are about to find love of their own!

Love and God bless,

# Chapter One

Emily Dunn bolted upright in the bed. Her heart was thundering in her chest and nothing about the dark room felt familiar.

Jerking her head to the right, she saw a row of curtained windows. Back to the left, her eyes fixed on a nightstand. There, beneath a table lamp, the red glowing numbers of a digital alarm clock glared twelve forty-five.

Slowly her senses began to right themselves and everything came rushing back to her. The accident. The funeral. The awful realization that her husband was never coming back.

Swinging her legs over the side of the mattress, she reached for a robe lying at the end of the bed. It was a cold October night, but whatever had awakened her so abruptly had left her sweating beneath her nightgown. She swiped a hand against her damp forehead, then stood on shaky legs to pull the burgundy velour robe over her bare arms and shoulders.

Knowing sleep was out of the question now, she headed to the kitchen to make herself a cup of cocoa and switch on the radio. Snow had been predicted in the mountains around Alto, Ruidoso, Lincoln and Hondo. An hour ago when she'd gone to bed, the sky over the ranch was low and gray, but no snow had yet fallen.

Halfway to the kitchen Emily stopped in her tracks. She was certain she'd heard a rattling noise outside. Perhaps something other than her troubled thoughts had interrupted her sleep? It could have been a piece of loose sheet iron whipping in the wind, but an inner feeling told her something or someone was out there.

Quickly tightening the sash of the robe around her waist, she hurried to the nearest window and pulled back the curtain. Throughout the ten years she'd lived on the Diamond D, she couldn't remember them ever having a prowler or anything stolen. But now that Kenneth was dead someone might view the place as easy pickings. The ranch was located on a lonely stretch of land north of the valley where the mountains turned to desert. Certainly no one came here unless they meant to.

The noise came again and this time Emily decided it was definitely the rattle of a stock trailer. What in the world was going on? Her father, Harlan, would never drive over here in the middle of the night unless it was an absolute emergency. At ten, she'd spoken to him briefly on the telephone and he'd been on his way to bed. As for the rest of her family, they would never show up in the middle of the night without calling first.

An uneasy chill swept through her as her mind began to spin. Her uncle Roy was the sheriff of Lincoln County. She could call him. But he and Aunt Justine lived a good thirty minutes away. She didn't want to disturb them unless it turned out to be a real emergency. Besides, if a thief was already out there, he could drive off with a whole trailer load of cows and horses by the time the law could get here.

Her jaw grimly set, she walked quietly but quickly back to the bedroom and took a .30.30 rifle down from a rack on the wall. A box of bullets was in the nightstand. Her heart tripping over itself, she loaded the rifle full, then jacked a shot into the barrel. She didn't intend to shoot anyone. But she wouldn't hesitate to scare the hell out of them.

Rifle in one hand, she pulled on a pair of cowboy boots, then dropped a cellular phone into the pocket of her robe. If she did find more trouble than she could handle outside, she would at least be able to call her uncle Roy for help.

Moments later, she slipped soundlessly from a door at the back of the house. Wind was blowing from the north and Emily realized the mist stinging her face was actually bits of snow too fine to see in the dark.

Shivering from cold and fear, Emily made her way to the corner of the house, then carefully peeped around the edge toward the barn. The yard lamp at the corner of the corrals would normally have illuminated the front of the barn, but the light had been broken for months. What little moonlight there might have been was blotted out by the clouds. The most she could discern was the back of a two-horse trailer.

Realizing she had no one but herself to handle things, Emily stepped away from the shadow of the house and moved stealthily toward the barn.

Whoever had driven here was more than likely in the barn, looking for saddles or tack to steal, she decided. A good saddle was always worth several hundred dollars. Especially if the saddle had been handmade as were the ones on the Diamond D. She'd be damned before she'd let some-one take them!

Inching forward, she could see the club cab pickup pull-ing the horse trailer. It was a fairly late model with Texas plates. This thief was obviously a long way from home. Not to mention traveling in style.

She was creeping closer to the open doorway of the barn when suddenly a light flared on inside the building. Stopping dead in her tracks, she held her breath and waited. Only a bold thief would turn on a light.

A few more seconds passed. A horse nickered, but nothing else stirred. With sudden decision, she stepped into the open doorway of the barn, the rifle aimed and ready.

"Who's in there?" she called loudly. "Come out or I'm going to shoot!"

Two horses Emily had never seen before were tied to the top rail of a nearby stall. Both animals, a bay and a gray, skittered nervously at the sound of her raised voice.

To the left of her, hinges creaked. Her head twisted in the direction of the sound and her heart beat like a drum in her throat as she watched the door to the feed room slowly swing forward. When the man finally stepped out and into the dim light, she stared in shock as the room seemed to tilt around her.

"Cooper? Is that you?"

The man slowly pushed the brim of his Stetson back off his forehead, then turned to face Emily head-on. Inclining his head toward the .30.30, he asked, "Is that the way you greet people on the Diamond D now, or just me?"

It suddenly dawned on her that she was still pointing the barrel of the rifle straight at him. Lowering the weapon, she drew in a bracing breath and took a couple of shaky steps toward her brother-in-law.

"No one prowls around in my barn at this time of night. What are you doing here?"

Cooper didn't miss the *my* in her answer or anything else about the woman standing a few steps away from him. It had been a long time since he'd seen her. Ten years to be exact. Yet he would have known her in a crowd a thousand miles away from this place.

"This was as soon as I could get here."

Emily hadn't expected him to get here at all. And the fact that he had stunned her ability to think, to do anything but continue to stare at him. Slowly and purposely her eyes took in everything between his brown boots and gray hat.

He looked as he had ten years ago, she decided, only a little older. His hair was still a tangle of sable brown curls against the back of his neck. Beneath the gray down jacket he wore, she could glimpse his trim waist and muscled thighs. If he'd put any weight on his six foot frame, she couldn't see it.

Cooper had never looked anything like his brother Kenneth, who'd been blond with a heavier build and smooth, almost classical features. The difference in the two men struck her even more as her gaze settled on his lean face. Cooper could not be called a handsome man. The bone structure of his face was roughly chiseled, his lips thin and his eyes hooded. Yet put all together he had a striking, masculine appearance. One that she had certainly never been able to forget.

"Kenneth's funeral was two days ago," she said bluntly.

His gray eyes caught and held her blue ones. "I figured as much. But the news of his accident didn't catch up to me until yesterday. I've been driving ever since."

If that was supposed to make her feel better, it didn't. His few hours on the road to get here didn't make up for ten years of neglect.

"I really don't know why you bothered to come at all."

Cooper's gaze slid over the silk curtain of blond hair lying against Emily's shoulders, the slender curves of her body beneath the heavy robe. She had to be thirty-five or six now. The same age as himself. Yet she looked far younger. And oh so achingly beautiful.

"Kenneth was my brother. That's why I bothered."

So he wasn't here because of her. Emily had known that, but hearing him say it cut her anyway. Which was ridiculous. Cooper had never really cared for her. She'd known that for a long time now.

Gripping the rifle, she said, "I'm cold. I'm going in. Are you staying here tonight?"

Her question brought a twist to his lips. "You might not think so, but the Diamond D is still my home."

Her brows arched with disbelief. He'd not stepped foot on the Diamond D once in ten years. She couldn't see how he could still consider it his home. As far as she knew, the man didn't have a home.

"That's debatable," she said stiffly, then turning to go, she tossed over her shoulder, "I'll make you up a bed."

"Emily."

Pausing at the door she looked back at him. The moment her eyes connected with his, warm, sweet memories flooded her mind and brought searing tears to her throat. She wanted to run straight to him and cry her heart out against his chest. It was a shocking, reckless feeling that overwhelmed her with guilt. Yet it was there inside her just the same.

"I just wanted to say…I'm very sorry about Kenneth."

And so was she. For so many reasons. "Me too, Cooper."

She left the barn and Cooper turned back to his horses. And in that moment he realized he'd never felt more alone in his life.

Fifteen minutes later he found Emily in the kitchen. She was still in the robe and cowboy boots, but thankfully the rifle was nowhere in sight.

Shrugging out of his jacket, he hung it and his hat on a peg by the door, then turned and let his eyes drink in a room that had once been so much a part of his life. Other than the curtains on the windows and the Formica table being replaced with a wooden one, it looked the same as Cooper remembered.

Though the room was bare now he could easily imagine what it had looked like two days ago when they'd buried his brother. The kitchen had probably been crammed with friends and distant relatives. All sorts of food dishes would have lined the cabinets and tables. There had surely been lots of tears and hugs meant to comfort, and talk about what a good man Kenneth had been, and how tragic it was for him to have been killed in the prime of life.

Cooper was actually glad he hadn't been here. He could do without all those people with their endless questions and pointed looks. Without having to ask, he knew people around here considered him the black sheep of the Dunn family. The prodigal son who'd waited too late to come home.

"I'm making cocoa. Would you like a cup?" she asked, breaking the silence.

The room was cold. He drew closer to her and the cookstove. "Yes. It's been a few hours since I've eaten."

Not trusting herself to look at him, she motioned with her head toward the refrigerator. "There's plenty of leftovers if you want to dig them out."

In other words she wasn't going to bother feeding him. Well, Cooper hadn't expected her to go out of her way to see to his comforts. But he had planned on her being a little bit warmer than this.

"The cocoa will be enough," he told her.

Her eyes remained fixed on the saucepan of milk as she stirred it back and forth with a hypnotic rhythm. In the brighter light of the kitchen, Cooper could see the lines of fatigue on her face, the deep bruises of lost sleep beneath her eyes.

He'd expected to find her grieving. After all, Kenneth had been her husband for nearly ten years. Yet the longer he studied her, he decided she was more weary than anything.

"I was in east Texas yesterday. Before that, Montana. I'm sorry I missed Kenneth's funeral."

Emily doubted the sincerity of his words. Yet he was

here now. She should at least give him credit for making any sort of appearance, she decided.

"The eulogy was very nice. The church was packed—even some of my old accounting clients came—and I've never seen so many flowers."

Her voice was wooden and Cooper wondered if she was deliberately making it so to keep from breaking down in front of him.

"I'm glad for that much at least. Can you tell me what happened? The message I got only stated that Kenneth had been killed by a fall from a horse. Is that right?"

The cocoa was bubbling around the edges. Emily carried the pan over to the cabinet counter and filled two large mugs. At the end of the table she placed a mug for him, then sat down with her own.

"You know how Kenneth never would let a horse get the better of him," she began. "But this one was mean all the way through. I'd begged him to get rid of it but—" Her eyes on the mug in her hands, she shrugged. "He didn't listen to me."

Cooper joined her at the table. "Was this a green horse he was breaking?"

It seemed incredible to Emily that she was sitting here talking to him as if he'd never really been away. As if nothing had ever happened between them. Down through the years she'd imagined him coming home so many times and how it might feel to see him again. Yet none of her imaginings came close to the strange mixture of pain and joy surging through her at this moment.

"No. It wasn't a young horse he was just breaking," she answered. "He used the gelding to work cattle and ride fence line. But the animal was temperamental and Kenneth had to watch him every second. The day he…I'd gone into Ruidoso and he'd planned to go check on a bull he'd been doctoring. We don't really know what happened. It appeared the horse spooked for some reason and started bucking. Kenneth fell and it snapped his neck.''

Cooper drew in a deep breath, then let it out slowly. His brother had always been a good rider. But even the best of horsemen got caught off guard at times. He knew that as well as anyone.

"Are you the one who found him?"

She shook her head. "I was out looking for him. Along with my dad and Uncle Roy and several of his deputies. Daddy was the one who found him."

He sipped the cocoa and rubbed a hand through his dark hair. "It's hard to picture Kenneth not being able to handle a horse. He was always so good with them."

In spite of Cooper's long absence from the Diamond D, Emily could see he was feeling a loss for his brother. Her heart almost softened toward him. Almost, but not quite.

"It wasn't really the horse that killed him. It was the liquor," she said bluntly.

Cooper's gray eyes narrowed on her pale face. "Liquor? What are you talking about? My brother never drank."

Glancing away from him, she lifted the mug of cocoa to her lips. After she'd managed to take a couple of swallows, she asked, "How do you know?"

Rage at the loss of his brother, his home, and all that had happened ten years ago surged up in his craw like bitter acid. "Kenneth was your husband, but he was also my brother," he said stonily. "I knew him."

The bit of compassion she'd felt for him a moment ago vanished. "Yeah. Back when? Before you became a big rodeo star? Well, I'm sorry, Cooper, but the brother you knew wasn't the one that fell from a horse and broke his neck."

Something flickered in his gray eyes. Doubt? Guilt? Whatever it was sliced into Emily like the edge of a rusty razor.

"What are you trying to say? Had Kenneth become an alcoholic?" he asked.

She realized what her words were probably doing to him. Cooper had always looked up to his older brother. From what he'd once told her, Kenneth had been a steadying influence to him after their parents had died. Then later, when Cooper had decided to try his hand at bronc riding, Kenneth had urged him on like a proud papa. If either of the Dunn brothers had possessed a wild streak, it had been Cooper, not Kenneth.

Emily's blue eyes were suddenly snapping with anger as she looked at him and it dawned on Cooper this was the most emotion he'd seen on her face since he'd arrived.

"No. Kenneth wasn't an alcoholic, but it was in the makings. I told him not to ever get on that horse if he'd been drinking. But he did anyway. A man with drunk reflexes shouldn't be on a gentle nag, much less a loco cow horse."

Cooper felt physically ill. When the news of Kenneth's death had reached him all he could think was what a senseless way to die. But now—what Emily was telling him made it far worse. "You know for a fact Kenneth had been drinking? You'd said you were gone to Ruidoso. You couldn't have seen him."

Emily pushed aside her unfinished cocoa and got up from the table. "The autopsy report stated there was enough alcohol in his bloodstream to make him well past the legal point of drunkenness. I'm sorry, Cooper, but that's the way it was."

He stared up at her in disbelief. "You're sorry!"

Before she could make a reply, he jumped to his feet and grabbed her by the upper arm. "That's all you can say, you're sorry?" His face bore down on hers. "What the hell were you thinking, Emily? Why did you let him get on a horse in such a condition? What were you doing?"

Her features cold and stiff, she ripped her arm from his grasp. "What were *you* doing, Cooper?"

Her pointed question stunned him. His hand fell away from her arm, but his gray eyes mercilessly held onto hers.

The sick look on his face didn't give Emily any pleasure and she decided they had both said enough for one night. None of it mattered anyway. Kenneth was gone. And so would Cooper, too. Probably by the end of the day.

Turning away from him, she started out of the room. Before she reached the door, she said, "I made up the bed in your old room. If you want any breakfast, I'll have it ready by seven."

Cooper wanted to call her back, but he didn't. It was late and he could see she was exhausted. Now wasn't the time to press her about his brother. But he would before he left here. And he'd make damn sure he got some answers.

The next morning Emily was frying bacon when Rose, her stepmother, called. Holding the portable phone with one hand, she forked the frying bacon with the other.

"I'm just checking on you," Rose said. "Did you sleep last night?"

Emily closed her eyes and tried to swallow the lump in her throat. For twenty-three years Rose had been her mother in every sense of the word and throughout that time her love and gentle kindness had never wavered. Nor had it ever failed to touch Emily's heart.

"A little," she told her.

Picking up the weariness in her voice, Rose said, "You need more than a little sleep. Your dad is going to the horse sale with a friend so I've got the day to myself. Why don't you go back to bed after you eat and I'll come over and see to the chores for you."

"You did that yesterday," Emily reminded her.

"And it didn't hurt me one little bit. Now tell me if you need me to bring you anything and I'll be over in an hour or so."

Emily dropped a piece of bacon onto a plate lined with

paper towels. "No," she said quickly. "Don't do that. I'll be fine."

"But honey, I want to help you."

"I know," she said, then decided she should explain. "Cooper came home last night."

The line went quiet as Rose digested her daughter's abrupt news. "Is he there now?"

Emily glanced over her shoulder to make sure the man hadn't slipped into the kitchen without her knowing. "Yes."

"How long does he plan to stay?"

"He hasn't said and I haven't asked."

Rose went silent for another long spell. "How does he seem to be taking Kenneth's death?"

"I think he's still in a bit of shock about it." And Emily was still in a shock over seeing Cooper again.

"Well, I know the two of them were close at one time. But frankly, I'm surprised the news brought Cooper home. He's never bothered before. And what can he do now?"

"I've been thinking the very things you just said."

"So you don't really know his intentions?" Rose asked.

"Not yet."

Rose groaned. "Oh Lord, Emily, I wished the man had stayed gone. Harlan isn't going to like this one little bit. He hasn't forgotten how Cooper hurt you. And if he's come back with plans to take over his half of the ranch—well, all I can say is I see trouble."

*His half of the ranch.* Like a cold north wind, the words rushed through Emily. It was true that Cooper and Kenneth had shared ownership of the ranch since their father had died fifteen years ago. But Cooper had never seen fit to take any interest in the place. Neither with money nor his presence. She couldn't see that changing just because Kenneth was no longer here.

"You're borrowing trouble, Mom. Cooper doesn't have any intentions toward the Diamond D. Why would he? He's a big rodeo star now. He has all the money he needs. And anybody with one good eye can see this place is falling down around my ears. No. You can rest assured Cooper couldn't be bothered.''

''I hope you're right, darling. You have enough on your mind without something like that. You haven't told him anything, have you?''

Emily switched off the burner beneath the skillet and took a peep in the oven at the baking biscuits. ''What do you mean? About the accident?''

''No. About you.''

Emily quickly glanced over her shoulder again. A few minutes before her mother had called, she'd heard Cooper head down the hall to the bathroom. Any second now she expected him to walk into the kitchen.

''I have no intentions of telling him anything about my condition. It's none of his business. And I'd appreciate it if you'd tell Daddy and the rest of the family not to say anything if they happen to run into Cooper.''

''Is there a reason you don't want him to know?''

She bit down on her lip as several reasons came to mind. ''He…doesn't need to know, that's all. Now I've got to finish breakfast. I'll call you later, Mom.''

''All right, honey, if that's the way you feel. You know your daddy and I are here if you need us.''

Knowing she had her parents' support was one of the things that had kept her going. ''And I love you for it. We'll talk later.''

She placed the phone out of the way then gathered a couple of pot holders and pulled the pan of hot bread from the oven.

''Something smells good. Is it biscuits?''

Emily glanced around just as Cooper walked into the room. Even though she knew he'd slept across the hall from her last night, it was still a shock to the senses to see him this morning.

He hadn't shaved but she could see he must have taken a quick shower because his dark hair was wet and slicked back from his face. A red plaid shirt hung half buttoned on the outside of his jeans. His feet were bare except for a pair of white socks.

"Yes, it's biscuits. And you shouldn't be walking around without your boots. The floor is gritty. You'll ruin your socks."

He gave her a twisted smile. "I've been known to get grit in my boots before."

No doubt, she thought. He'd made his living in thousands of dusty rodeo arenas. It shouldn't matter to her if he ruined ten pair of socks on her dirty floors. And it shouldn't feel so good to look at him, either. But it did.

Carrying the pan of biscuits over to the table, she motioned for him to take a seat at one of the empty plates. "How do you want your eggs? Scrambled or fried?"

"Fried, if it isn't too much trouble."

She went to the stove, broke four eggs into a skillet of warm grease, then carried a coffeepot back to the table and filled his cup.

"Are you always up and going this early?" he asked.

She glanced at the clock on the wall. "Normally I'm up and about much earlier. But I've tried to get a little more rest these past few days." Not that laying in bed an hour and a half more did any good, she thought. She still felt drained and groggy, but she was determined to get better, to be able to smile and laugh again.

"You look tired."

As she tended the cooking eggs, her free hand unconsciously fluttered to her bare cheek. With no makeup and her hair pulled back in a messy French braid she knew she must look awful. Her work jeans and old blue sweater didn't help matters, either. But for the past couple of years, she'd ceased to think of her appearance as important. How irritating for Cooper to notice and point out such a thing to her.

"Ten years can do a lot to a person's looks."

He picked up the steaming cup of coffee and savored the smell as he brought it to his lips. After a careful sip, he said, "I didn't say you looked older. I said you looked tired."

The eggs done, she carried the skillet over to the table, ladled three onto his plate and one on her own.

As she took a seat opposite him, her eyes briefly met his and she wondered, if like her, he was remembering back to the breakfasts they shared ten years ago.

Emily hoped not. She hoped that once he'd left the Diamond D, he'd totally forgotten the unabashed way she'd loved him, the nights she'd spent cradled in his strong arms. Just thinking of the pleasure he'd given her sent a shaft of guilty heat rushing through her.

"I'm really okay," she told him.

Emily didn't look okay. She looked like hell, but Cooper kept the opinion to himself. He could see her nerves were raw and he hadn't come here to the Diamond D to cause her more pain. In all honesty, Cooper wasn't exactly sure why he'd come back.

The funeral had already taken place. He couldn't help his brother now and he didn't necessarily want to assert himself into Emily's life just because she was his sister-in-law and newly widowed. Nor did he figure she would appreciate him sticking his nose into any unfinished legal business she might have to deal with over the accident. So had he really come here just to see her one more time? He didn't want to answer that.

Shaking tabasco over his eggs, he asked, "How is everyone else around here? Do your parents still live on the Flying H?"

Relieved that he wasn't going to bring up Kenneth's accident right off, she relaxed a little. "Yes. My brother Ethan has graduated college and is living back home now."

His brows lifted and for the first time since she'd found him in the barn last night there was a genuine smile on his face. "Little Ethan is out of college? Why, he was just a little ornery horned toad that last time I saw him."

A vague tilt to her lips, she passed him a biscuit then took one for herself. "Well, he's all grown up now."

"What about your aunts?"

"Justine and Chloe are fine. So are their children. Uncle Roy is still the sheriff. He thought about retiring last year, but the people in this county love him too much to let him go. And my cousin Charlie loves being a Texas Ranger. Uncle Wyatt is still in the oil business and of course Daddy will always be a rancher."

And what about you, he wanted to ask her. Had she been happy as Kenneth's wife? Really happy? Cooper knew he had no right to put those questions to her. But for the past ten years he'd thought of little else.

"What about your other cousins? Are they still living around here?"

"The twins are all grown up now. Anna is touring as a concert pianist and Adam is working in the gas business with his dad. Their younger sister, Ivy, is at NMU studying to be a doctor. And you remember Charlie's younger sister, Caroline. She lives in Santa Fe and works as a jewelry designer. None of them have married yet. I guess they've all been too busy building their careers."

Wishing he could think about anything but her, he turned his attention to the food on his plate. It tasted good and he was hungry. But the eggs and bacon did little to fill up the empty hole in him.

"Emily," he began after a few minutes of silence. "Last night…about Kenneth…if I sounded—"

When it appeared he couldn't find the words to go on, Emily did it for him. "Out of line?"

He didn't necessarily think his question had been out of line. Still, he did feel a little badly about being so rough on her. But hell, she'd met him with the barrel of a .30.30 pointed straight at his gut. The greeting hadn't exactly put him in a warm mood.

"I don't think wanting to know how my brother died was asking too much. Even if you didn't want to talk about it."

She reached for her coffee, but suddenly the smell of it sickened her. She put the cup down and reached for the orange juice she'd poured earlier.

"You think I'm to blame because Kenneth is dead," she said flatly. "You think I should have stopped him somehow."

He grimaced. "I didn't—"

"You said it. You know you did. So don't be bashful. Tell me what you're really thinking now. God knows I can take it."

That weariness was back in her voice and Cooper realized he hated it. More than anything he wanted to see the warm, vibrant Emily he used to know.

"Okay. I know that if there was one person on this earth who could have prevented Kenneth from getting on that horse, it was you."

The smile she gave him was so utterly sad he could hardly bear to look at her. "At one time, that might have been true. But not now."

"Why was Kenneth drinking?"

She couldn't finish the food on her plate. In fact, she was going to be lucky if she didn't lose what little she'd managed to get down.

"Why does anyone drink?" she countered. "He was unhappy with me, the ranch, life in general."

Cooper didn't want to believe what she was saying. Kenneth had never been a down person. It had always taken so little to make him happy. He couldn't imagine his brother changing so drastically.

Seeing the doubt and confusion on his face, Emily said, "I wasn't having an affair, if that's what you're thinking. And as far as I know, Kenneth wasn't cheating on me. He was—well, he'd changed the last few years. I don't know what he wanted and apparently whatever it was, I couldn't give it to him." She lifted her eyes to his. "So maybe you are right. Maybe I did cause his death."

"Oh hell, Emily. That's not what I needed to hear you say."

Her brows inched slowly upward. "Then what do you want to hear from me?"

Suddenly he couldn't face her. Too many bittersweet memories of the times he and Emily had spent together were pouring in over the pain he was already feeling for Kenneth.

With a little groan he got up from the table and walked over to a door that led out to the backyard. Through the windowpanes, he could see a part of the barn and the adjoining corrals. It was a pitiful sight. Much worse than he'd suspected it to be last night. Boards were rotting, fences were sagging, sheets of tin were loose and flopping in the cold wind. It was a far cry from the ranch he remembered as his home.

"I guess I just wanted to hear that my brother was happy. But it seems as though you can't even give me that much."

She looked down at her plate and blinked. It was the closest she'd come to crying since she'd first set eyes on him last night. Cooper had once been everything to her. When she thought of the word happy, she always thought of him.

"Your world might be a beautiful place, Cooper. But here on the Diamond D things have been…tough."

Folding his arms across his chest, he turned to face her. "Then why are you here?"

The sight of him standing there so strong and handsome and alive infuriated her. He'd turned his back on her, broke her heart and virtually shunned his brother. He had no right to show his face here again, much less interrogate her!

Shoving her chair back from the table she marched over to within inches of him. "Because it's my home, Cooper. But that's something you wouldn't understand. You don't want a home. And from the looks of you, I doubt you'll ever have one!"

A sneer twisted his lean face. "If this is what you call a home, I'm damn glad I don't!"

Suddenly everything Emily had been through since she'd first met Cooper Dunn came whirling through her like an angry tornado. All she could see was him leaving and never coming back.

It was the stinging pain in her hand that finally jolted Emily back to reality. Instantly, anger and horror swept across her face. She'd slapped him!

Rubbing the wounded spot on his jaw, Cooper eyed her flushed cheeks. "So there is life in you after all."

Oh God, he didn't know. He couldn't know!

Pressing her hand over her mouth, she ran to the bathroom and prayed he wouldn't hear her retching.

# Chapter Two

On the edge of a windswept break, Cooper reined the gray to a halt and gazed out at the snowy mesa floor. Many times in the past he'd ridden to this very spot where the sagebrush grew belly high to a horse and a lone piñon pine stood sentinel over the ranch below.

However, this morning Cooper felt no joy as he looked down at the home that had been in the Dunn Family for more than a hundred years. The Diamond D was not the same. Not physically nor spiritually and the knowledge saddened him greatly.

He hadn't expected it to touch him like this. Hell, it had been years since he'd been on the place. He'd figured once he'd seen it again, the old ranch wouldn't mean that much to him. After all, it had always been Kenneth's baby. Their father had seen to that. William Dunn had never hidden the fact that of his two sons he considered Kenneth to be the better rancher. It was one of the main reasons Cooper had worked so hard to succeed at bronc riding. He'd never felt as if he really had a place of importance here on the ranch.

Yet in spite of all that, it cut something deep inside him to see the home place like this. So shabby. So empty.

Pushing his coat collar up against the falling snow, Cooper nudged the gray down the bluff and back toward the house. Smoke was spiraling up from the old rock chimney, signaling him that Emily had just stoked up the fire.

Unconsciously his fingertips touched the spot on his jaw she'd slapped. The memory of her anger this morning put a wry smile on his lips. Emily was still Emily after all, and he wondered how she was going to react when he told her what he planned to do.

Almost a half hour later, Cooper found her in the living room in front of the fireplace. The rocking chair she sat in was an old oak one that had belonged to his mother. The back was high and the arms and legs carved. Though he'd never known his mother, others had told him the chair had been a favorite of Laura Dunn's and it comforted Cooper somehow to see Emily in it now.

"The snow is getting heavier," he said as he grew near her and the warm fire.

She glanced up from the blue jeans she was patching to see him shedding a heavy sheepskin coat. Snow still clung to his shoulders and the brim of his hat. His nose and cheeks were reddened by the cold wind. She wondered why he'd bothered to go out on such a nasty morning.

"It's only the end of October," she replied. "I hope this isn't a forewarning to what the rest of the winter is going to be like."

Taking a seat in a stuffed armchair a few feet away from her, his eyes wandered over the room. Other than being run-down, it really hadn't changed much in appearance, either. The ceiling was low and traversed with dark oak beams, the walls white plaster, the floor Spanish tile. The house was typical hacienda style and in its early years had once been regarded as a showcase. Now it needed money and a complete refurbishment. As did everything else he looked at on the place.

His eyes coming to rest on her face, he said, "I didn't see much hay stacked away in the barn. Is that all you have?"

She nodded. "That's it. Kenneth didn't want to bother planting an alfalfa crop."

His features twisted with confusion. "What the hell did he plan to feed this winter?"

Emily grimaced and placed her mending on the floor beside the rocker. "When our alfalfa ran out, he'd planned on buying more hay from Daddy. It would be cheaper that way. Especially with Daddy giving us a generous cut."

"That doesn't sound like Kenneth."

Her expression both wry and sad, she glanced over at him. "No. Not the Kenneth you used to know."

"For as long as I can remember the Diamond D raised its own alfalfa. It was one of the reasons why the ranch did so well."

She looked back at the fire while thinking how ironic to hear Cooper repeating all the old arguments she'd given Kenneth. "I know. But the tractor has been giving us lots of problems. Kenneth figured by the time we fixed it, then counted the cost of fertilizer, labor and baling, we'd be better off not raising a crop of hay."

Scooting to the edge of the chair, Cooper leaned toward her. "I'm going to tell you flat out, Emily. This place looks like hell. What's been going on?"

Emily had figured that once daylight came, and Cooper had the chance to look around the place, he was going to be appalled. The ranch looked nothing like the one he'd known before he left for the rodeo circuit.

Rising from the rocker, she stood with her back to the warmth of the fire. "You've been here a few hours and you want to hear in one short explanation what's happened to the ranch," she said dryly.

Cooper's gray eyes drifted up and down the length of her. She was a tall woman and from the looks of her, age hadn't added any extra pounds to her slender frame. If anything, she appeared thinner. But it was difficult for Cooper to really tell much about her shape beneath the baggy jeans and sweater she was wearing.

"Do you not want to tell me? Or do you just not know? Which one is it?" he asked.

He sounded outraged and Emily stared at him in disbelief. "In the ten years you've been gone, you've never wondered or worried about the ranch's condition. Don't you think your display of concern is a little late in coming?"

Her sarcasm made Cooper want to go to her and shake her. But her fragile appearance stopped him. He got the feeling if he touched her, she just might break.

"Ever since Dad died, the Diamond D has been in Kenneth's hands. That's the way he wanted it," he said quietly. "My brother would have never let it get in this condition without a reason."

Lifting her eyes to the ceiling, Emily let out a long sigh. "A reason? Why not several reasons?"

"Okay. So there was more than one. Tell me."

Her mind said she didn't owe this man any explanations. He'd forfeited everything when he'd walked away. Yet when she looked at him, her heart interfered with her thinking. Kenneth had been his brother and this had been his home. It couldn't be easy for him to find them both gone.

"Cooper, the ranch's decline happened over years. Little by little Kenneth seemed to lose interest. And then all sorts of problems kept popping up, like broken-down vehicles, sick cows, bad weather. The list goes on. But I guess the plummeting price in the cattle market is what finally broke the place."

His brows shot up. "The ranch is broke?"

She supposed that was hard for a man like him to imagine. Through the gossip grapevine and what little bit of sports news she caught on TV, she knew Cooper Dunn had made plenty of money these past ten years riding broncs in the PRCA. He was a champion, a celebrity figure in the world of rodeo. His finances had done nothing but grow.

"Let me put it this way. The ranch isn't making money."

"How many cattle are you running now?" he asked.

"A hundred and fifty head."

The amount was so paltry she might as well as said none. He looked at her and the disgust on his face brought a flush of anger to her cheeks.

"I know it sounds and looks bad," she told him, "but when you have a bad streak of luck—"

"You get up and fight back," he interrupted hotly. "You don't lose interest and you sure as hell don't start drinking!"

"I didn't do either of those things," she retorted. "Nor do I plan to."

But Kenneth had. She couldn't have made it any plainer to him. But the ranch was still here. Barely. Cooper couldn't let it die, too.

Rising from the chair, he went to stand beside her. She looked up at him as his shoulder came close to nudging hers and as Cooper searched her azure blue eyes he realized he'd forgotten nothing about this woman. Her honey pale skin, the length of her pert little nose, the curve of her full lips. Lips that he'd kissed whenever the urge had struck him. And the urge had struck him often. To his dismay, it still was.

"I was planning on leaving this evening. Along with the bronc riding, I've started competing in the team roping and I'm drawn in a rodeo in Arizona two days from now. But I'm not going."

Aghast, she whispered, "Not going?"

Glancing away from her, he shook his head. Emily's already jumpy stomach took a nosedive. "Why? I'm sure there's several more rodeos for you to make between now and the National Finals in December.''

''Eight at least. But they'll manage to go on without me.''

Maybe, Emily thought. But she wasn't at all sure she could survive with him here. All she had to do was look at him and she remembered everything about him. The taste of his skin, the flash of his smile, the sweet bliss of his body next to hers. Oh God, it wasn't right for her to think of such things with Kenneth barely gone. But she couldn't stop herself. She'd never been able to stop herself.

Turning her gaze to the fire, she asked, ''Why would you possibly want to stay? There's nothing for you here.''

At one time Cooper had thought there was plenty for him here because she was here. He'd hoped and planned to eventually come back a rich man, a man worthy to be Emily's husband. But she hadn't waited. She'd married Kenneth instead. Even now, after all these years, the knowledge stabbed him deep and hard.

''Unless things have changed more than I know, I'm still part owner of this place,'' Cooper stated coolly. ''I have a right to see that my own property is taken care of. Or were you planning on selling it and moving into Ruidoso or somewhere else in this area?''

His question put a blank look on her face. ''Sell?'' she echoed. ''I'd never do that. Besides, as you said, you're half owner. I couldn't sell without your consent.''

It really didn't make any sort of sense, but it was a great relief to Cooper to hear her say she had no notions to sell the Diamond D. Selling would probably be the smart thing to do. She was a woman alone, without the funds to get the place going again. With what money they could get out of the property, she would have enough to start a new home somewhere and he could go on back to his rodeo life and not have the burden of the ranch on his mind.

But the Diamond D had always belonged to a Dunn. His

father had been born here and he'd died here. So had his grandfather. The Dunn men had carved this ranch right out of Apache land. Back then, water had been as precious as gold and the Lincoln county range war had turned the desert plains into a bloody battlefield. It was even rumored that during those days of the 1870s, Cooper's great-grandfather Dunn had rode with the great rancher, John Tunstall, and rubbed shoulders with Billy the Kid.

Whether that part of the family history was true or not, Cooper couldn't really say. But he did know for more than a century, a Dunn had ranched this land. How could he walk away from that?

"Cooper, is that what you want? You want to sell the Diamond D?"

Her voice finally penetrated his deep thoughts. "I'm sorry," he said, swiping a weary hand over his face. "Were you asking me something?"

She repeated her questions and he quickly shook his head.

"No. I don't want to sell the ranch."

Her mind spinning, Emily's gaze clung to his hard face. "But you can't want to stay here!"

His gray eyes cut down to hers and once again, memories swamped her. No man, including her husband, had gotten as close to her as Cooper had. When she'd been in his arms, the rest of the world had faded away. Nothing had mattered but him and having him close. If he stayed on the Diamond D she'd be so tempted...so crazy all over again.

"Why?"

"Because this isn't the way you want to live! You've got a career. And anyway, I live here alone. It wouldn't look...right if you were to stay in the house with me."

His lips twisting with wry amusement, he went over to the window and glanced outside. "I don't really see any neighbors out there watching us."

"Don't be flip. You know I have friends and family

around here. They'll all think it rather odd, don't you think? A brother-in-law moving in with his freshly widowed sister-in-law.''

"Moving in,'' he repeated with a snort. "You make it sound like we're two lovers who can't wait to set up housekeeping with each other.''

His sarcasm stung her and she shot him a disgusted look. "That's exactly the way it will sound to everybody else, too!''

Turning his back on her, Cooper stared out the murky windowpanes. He could feel cold air seeping around the wooden window frames, but the draft did little to cool his thoughts. Why did she have to remind him of how it had been to love her? She was his brother's widow and that's the way it had to stay.

"I don't give a damn what anyone else thinks!'' he said sharply. "This is between you and me. Like it or not, we own this ranch together. And I don't want to see it go under.''

If anyone could get the Diamond D going, Emily thought reluctantly, it would be Cooper. He might have been riding in the spotlight for the past ten years, but he knew ranching backward and forward. And from the looks of him, he had the energy to follow his ideas through. But what about the mental commitment? How long would it be before he was bored and ready to head back to Cheyenne or Calgary or San Antonio?

No, Emily decided. She didn't want him here. Especially with the baby coming. For so long she'd desperately wanted a child and now that she was finally pregnant she wanted to focus all her energy on carrying a healthy baby to full term. Cooper's presence would dredge up memories too painful to bear.

"I won't let the Diamond D go under. I promise you that,'' she told him.

He turned and stared at her. "What do you mean, you won't let it? It's already on its way."

She flushed. "Not totally. I still have a hundred and fifty head of cattle and ten head of horses."

His eyes quickly narrowed. "What about the horse that caused Kenneth's accident?"

She shook her head. "Daddy's already sold him."

He was visibly relieved. "Good. I didn't relish the idea of putting a horse down, but I would have."

Emily shook her head with disapproval. "As if that would do Kenneth any good now. An eye for an eye. A tooth for a tooth. A horse for a man. Is that your way of thinking?"

"Something like that."

"I can't imagine you laying one angry hand on a horse. You always loved them. And they you. I guess that's why they've made you rich and famous."

He walked toward her then and for a moment the smile spreading over his face made her forget he'd ever been gone.

"Who says I'm rich and famous?"

She shrugged, wishing she could keep quiet around this man. She didn't want him getting the idea he'd been in her thoughts down through the years. "Oh, everyone here in Lincoln, I suppose."

"Then everyone is wrong. I'm just one good cowboy out of many."

More than bothered by his closeness, Emily stepped off the hearth and away from him. "I'm going to go make a pot of coffee. It's nearly time for lunch and then I have to feed the cattle."

"Who's been doing your feeding?"

"My dad. But I told him not to come today. I want to take care of things myself and I can't do that moping around the house."

She didn't look strong enough to drive a pickup, much

less pitch a bale of hay off the back of it. But maybe her appearance was deceiving. Cooper certainly hoped that was the case.

He followed her out of the room and down the hall to the kitchen. Built on the north side of the house, the room was naturally colder than the others. Rubbing his hands together, Cooper went over to a gas heater on the wall and was dismayed to see it wasn't burning.

"Why don't you have the fire on? It's miserable in here," he muttered.

As Emily filled a blue granite percolator with cold water, she glanced over her shoulder at him. "A fire means gas and the cost of LP is outrageous now. If you're cold put more clothes on."

Emily had always been a practical woman, but this was ridiculous. "Damn it all, Emily, do you think I can't buy a tank of gas?"

He went over to the cabinets and jerked open a drawer he remembered being a catchall. Thankfully it still was and a box of matches was there among the odds and ends. He carried them back to the heater, lit it and turned the control knob to high position.

Her hands on her hips, Emily glared at him in silence. Cooper lifted his brows at her.

"I have on all the clothes I want to have on," he said.

"You might own half of this ranch, but I'm the one who pays the bills. I'm not going to buy extra gas just so you can sit around dressed like you're in the Bahamas."

Cooper glanced pointedly down at his flannel shirt. "I haven't seen too many of these on the beach before."

Whirling her back to him, she poured a stiff amount of coffee grounds into the pot, then plopped the lid down and whammed the whole thing on a burner on the cookstove.

"Emily, I just told you I can pay for the gas. It's no problem."

"I'll not have you paying for anything! Not while there's breath in my body," she hissed, her back still to him.

The venom in her voice stunned him. He'd expected her to be harboring a few bad feelings toward him. But not this bad.

"You'd rather freeze and keep your pride, I suppose," he said, his voice heavy with sarcasm. "You'd rather sit around in a cold, drafty house and take the chance of getting bronchitis or pneumonia than take a few dollars from me."

A few dollars wouldn't fill the propane tank, Emily wanted to shout at him. It would take several hundred and he knew it. But now that he was so successful, maybe he considered that amount as next to nothing.

Turning, she lifted her eyes to his. "Look, Cooper, the minute you start paying part of the bills, you'll get the idea you can tell me what to do. I won't have that."

He threw up his hands in a helpless gesture. "I can't do anything for you, is that it?"

His voice was still edged with sarcasm, but she could hear something else in it, too. A need of sorts that made her heart want to weep. Ten years ago she would have given anything to have him concerned about her welfare. But he'd been too busy planning his own life and his own career. She'd been left high and dry and he'd never looked back until now. Did he honestly think she would want to accept anything from him after the pain he caused her?

Anger pushing her away from the cabinets, she went over to stand in front of him. "Buy the damn gas if you want. Just don't start giving me orders, understand?"

Seeing her intention to walk away, he grabbed her by the upper arm and dragged her back to him. Her bosom heaving, she glared up at him and tried to jerk away, but he wouldn't slacken his hold.

"You've grown as hard as nails, Emily. Why? Has your life here been that bad?"

Compared to the grip he had on her arm, his voice was soft. The sound of it caught at something inside Emily and she knew above all things now, she had to hold on to her composure. She could never let herself break down and admit to him that her marriage to Kenneth had grown into a painful one.

"I'm not being hard, Cooper. I'm being realistic."

His eyes gently roamed her upturned face and as they did he wondered what had happened to the soft, beautiful woman who dreamed and hoped and looked at life with stars in her eyes. And in that moment, he knew he'd give anything to see that woman again.

"I never thought I'd come back and find you like this," he murmured.

She swallowed as bittersweet emotions balled in her throat. "I never thought you'd come back, period," she countered.

Cooper didn't profess to know women. Down through the years he'd had little time for the opposite sex. He'd never really been around any of them enough to learn their likes and dislikes, what they were thinking and feeling. But at one time in his life, he'd known Emily. And as he took in the pain on her face, it struck him that Kenneth wasn't the one that had made her like this. He had.

"Emily, I—"

Before he could say another word, Emily tore loose from his grip and fled the room.

Cooper was still staring after her when the sound of the coffee boiling out the spout and onto the cookstove finally snared his attention.

He went over and adjusted the burner to a slow perk, then pulled a coffee mug out of the cupboard. Apparently Emily was no longer in the mood for coffee, or him.

But whether she wanted to or not, she was going to have to get in the mood for him, he thought grimly. Because there was no way in hell he was going to leave now.

A few minutes later, as Cooper was finishing his coffee, Emily returned to the kitchen. Except for two bright spots on her cheeks, she looked as white as bleached flour. A couple of old coats were thrown across her arm and tall rubber boots were on her feet.

Tossing one of the coats at him, she said, "You wanted to help. Put that on and come with me."

Unaffected by her order, he remained in his chair, his hands cradled around the coffee mug. "It's time for lunch."

"We can eat whenever we get back," she said in a clipped voice.

If she'd been a man, Cooper would have taken the coat and thrown it straight at her. As it was, he got up from his chair, snatched away the coat that was still on her arm and pushed her into a chair.

"We're going to eat. Now!"

"I'm not hungry," she retorted.

"It looks as though you're never hungry, but you're going to eat just the same," he snapped back at her.

Indignant, Emily watched him rummage through the shelves of the refrigerator. One by one he set out a plate of fried chicken, a bowl of potato salad, a container of baked beans and a saucer of sliced tomatoes.

At the cabinets he searched until he found two plates and forks, salt and pepper and a roll of paper towels. After pouring her a mugful of coffee, he refilled his own.

"Eat," he said as he took a seat to her left.

She glared at him. "I told you not to be giving me orders."

"I haven't paid any bills so the deal isn't on yet."

As far as Emily was concerned, the deal would never be on. But she filled her plate just the same and made an earnest attempt to eat.

Her aunt Justine was a registered nurse and she'd been stressing over and over to Emily just how important it was for her baby to get the proper nourishment in the early stages of development. Even if she didn't have much of an appetite, she would eat for her baby's sake. The child was the one ray of light she could look forward to, the very purpose of her being. She wouldn't let Cooper or anything jeopardize her pregnancy.

"I want to talk to you," she told him and when he looked at her with raised brows, she added, "Seriously."

"I'm already getting the urge to call you *Your Honor.* Just how much more serious do you want to get?"

A little smile slowly crossed her face. In spite of everything that had happened it was nice to see he hadn't lost his wit. It had been one of her favorite things about him. He'd always been able to make her laugh.

When she'd first met Cooper, he'd been sidelined from his bronc riding with a broken leg and had come home to the Diamond D to heal. He'd needed a nurse to help him with physical therapy and eventually, through a mutual friend, he'd learned Justine had worked as a therapist and didn't live all that far away.

When her aunt had driven out to the Diamond D to meet Cooper, she'd invited Emily to accompany her. From the first moment she'd laid eyes on him, she'd been awestruck. Not because he'd already started to make a name for himself in the world of rodeo. Athletes had never really impressed Emily all that much, even when they pitted their strength against a twelve-hundred-pound horse. But for some unexplainable reason, she'd felt an instant connection to Cooper, a pull like an electric force from which she couldn't break away.

That had been more than ten years ago. Now he was back sitting only a few inches away and here she was once again feeling that same pull toward him. She had to stop it, she firmly told herself. She couldn't let herself feel drawn to this man. He was a user. A heartbreaker. She didn't need him.

"I want you to rethink this idea you have about staying here on the Diamond D," she told him. "You only have a couple more months to go before the season ends and then you'll have a bit of time off after the National Finals in Las Vegas. At this late date, it doesn't make sense for you to sideline your career. You can always come back later and check on the ranch."

He shot her a skeptical look. "And what's going to happen during November and December? You can't keep this place going by yourself."

She lifted her chin proudly. "Most of it, I can. And Daddy is already checking on a man to help me with the heavier work. If you feel you just have to do something, you can contribute to his wages. Otherwise, you're going to lose a lot of money and possibly even your position in the PRCA standings."

Any other time Cooper would have agreed with her, even appreciated the common sense she was using toward both their predicaments. But oddly enough, the money he might win in the next couple of months, or his number one position in the money earned column, didn't really mean what it once had to Cooper. He could live without the glory, the stardom and the big paychecks.

"I'm not all that worried about the next two months of rodeos. I'm more concerned about getting things done around here. There's hardly enough hay for the horses, let alone the cattle. Fences are falling down. The roof on the barn is sagging in and God only knows what else needs to be repaired. You said it had taken years for the ranch to get in this run-down condition, well, it looks as though it's going to take quite a long time to fix it."

Emily knew he was right. And she should probably be glad he wanted to make things better. But she couldn't live in the same house with him. She wasn't strong enough to forgive or forget what he'd done to her. Even worse, she wasn't at all sure she had the strength or courage to resist him.

"You're right. It will. But wouldn't it make more sense for you to simply hire the work done?"

He shrugged while his eyes made a shrewd assessment of her face. "Actually, the idea of doing some good ol' outdoor manual labor appeals to me."

"Sure," she said with dry disbelief. "This from a man who earns his living in eight-second intervals."

Even though she was being calm enough and sensible enough, Cooper could see that Emily didn't want him here. She either hated him, he concluded, or she was actually worried about what others might think of them living in the same house together.

"You've made it obvious you don't want me here, Emily. And I'll tell you something else. I'm not all that sure I want to be here." His gray eyes pinned hers. "You and I aren't exactly two people who should be thrown together as partners. But like it or not, we are."

She put down her fork and crumpled her dirty napkin. "I can live with us both owning the ranch. As long as you're a silent partner."

He very nearly laughed and for a split second Emily wished that ten years had never passed and she was back in that time when she'd loved and laughed and hoped along with him.

"I never was good at keeping my mouth shut," he said, while shoveling the last of the potato salad from his plate. "But I'll consider your suggestion. Maybe we can work something out so you won't have to put up with me and I won't have to miss the last of the rodeo season."

Dear God, she silently prayed, maybe he was finally listening to her. Cooper had to understand the two of them weren't meant to be working partners or partners of any sort. He needed to leave here before the past came crashing in on both of them.

# Chapter Three

Minutes later at the hay barn, Cooper ordered Emily to stand to one side while he loaded the back of an old work truck with several bales of alfalfa and three hundred pounds of caked feed.

As she watched him lift the heavy bales of hay, she knew it was a job she shouldn't be doing. Especially with her history of miscarriage. But she wasn't about to let Cooper know any part of what had happened to her after he'd left the ranch. Today she would accept his help and be grateful for it and hopefully by tomorrow she could persuade him to leave the Diamond D in her care. Maybe he'd stay away for another ten years.

If anything, the snowfall had grown heavier. As the old truck jostled over a rutted track toward the feeding ground, the wipers struggled to scrape away the fat flakes of ice sticking to the windshield.

Any other time, Emily would have enjoyed seeing the sage and piñon decorated in white, but today she hardly noticed the falling snow. Cooper had distracted her to say the least.

"Are you cold?"

His question caused her to glance across the seat at him. "I'm okay."

He twisted the knob on the heater to a warmer setting. "Are you sure this heater even works? The air blowing from the defrost vents feels like it's coming off the north pole."

"What do you expect in this weather?"

He expected his brother would have a decent work truck with a heater. In bad weather it wasn't safe for a person to get this far away from the ranch without a source of heat.

"Everything on this damn place is about to fall apart!" he muttered.

Including her, Emily thought, as she huddled inside her old wool work coat and jammed her gloved hands between her legs.

"You've just gotten soft," she told him.

He snorted. "I admit I've been gone from this place for a long time, but since then I damn well haven't gone soft or lazy. Unlike somebody else around here."

Emily whipped around on the seat to face him. "If you're implying I have, then just keep your mouth shut! You don't know what I've been doing since you've been gone!"

His eyes bored into her. "Well, if you and Kenneth did all that much work, I sure as hell would like to see it. So far there's not a building, a shed or a fence on this property that looks as though it's had any attention in years!"

She didn't know why he'd suddenly gotten so angry. Just because the heater was lukewarm didn't warrant this sort of outburst from him.

"I told you Kenneth lost interest."

"What was he doing with his time?"

The dry look she shot him said, you ought to know. "He spent his time with the horses. Sorta like someone else who used to live here."

The sheepish expression stealing over his face told Emily she hadn't given him the answer he was expecting.

Muttering a curse under his breath, he braked the old truck to a halt. A short distance away were a group of wooden feed troughs sheltered from the north wind by a stand of juniper and piñon pine.

"You know," he said thoughtfully, "I keep wondering why you've hung around here for so long."

Emily quickly looked away from him and out the window. The cattle were several rises over from them, but the animals had heard the truck and were now making their way in a hungry trot toward the feed grounds.

"Like I told you this morning, I've hung around because this is my home. And Kenneth was my husband."

He studied the back of her old black hat and the blond braid lying against her ranch coat. The garment had once been dark brown but it had obviously been washed and worn until the color now resembled dead grass. Her hair was still beautiful, but it looked as though she'd trimmed it herself. Cooper wondered how long it had been since she'd spent time just for herself, doing those feminine things women do with their skin and hair and nails.

A faint scowl on his face, Cooper said, "It appears to me as if he wasn't being all that good of one. Or is that simply what you want me to believe?"

His question caused tears to collect in Emily's throat. More than anything she didn't want to belittle Kenneth to him. At one time the man had seemed to love her. And up until the past couple of years, he'd been a decent husband to her. It hadn't been his fault that she'd failed him somewhere along the way.

"Your brother was a good man," she said quietly. "He did...the best he could."

Before Cooper was able to respond, Emily climbed out of the truck and hurried around to the tailgate. She was reaching for a sack of feed when his hands came down on her shoulders.

"Move out of the way. I'll do this."

Digging in her boot heels, she twisted her head around enough to see his face. "You're supposed to be helping. Not giving orders."

"When did you get so damn stubborn?"

Her lips parted to answer, but suddenly his grip on her shoulders eased. The expression on his face softened and she forgot all about his question. For the first time in years, Cooper was touching her as though he really meant it and all Emily wanted to do was turn and bury her face in his chest, beg him to hold her and never let her go.

"Cooper, I—"

Troubled by the sudden charge of awareness between them, Cooper quickly thrust her aside and slung the fifty-pound sack of feed over his shoulder.

"If you want to do something, follow me and start spreading the cake while I get the other sacks," he said gruffly.

Relieved that he'd snapped her back to reality, Emily started after him. He set the sack of feed at one end of the nearest trough, then started to rip the string to open it.

"I'll do that," Emily quickly offered. "You go get the rest of the sacks before all the cattle get here. With this bit of snow on the ground they're going to be hungry and rowdy."

"Are any of them mean?"

"No," she assured him. "I promise you won't have to make a mad dash for the truck."

To Emily's surprise he grinned. "I'll keep an eye out anyway," he told her.

In a matter of moments the bawling steers reached the feed grounds and swarmed Emily. Working her way through the hungry cattle, she poured a long string of hard green pellets down the center of the wooden trough.

Once the sack was empty, she began walking to the next trough where Cooper had already placed another sack.

In their eagerness to be fed, the steers trotted ahead and around her. Emily pushed several animals out of her path, but before she was aware of the danger behind her she was sent sprawling to the ground.

The instant Cooper saw Emily fall, he tossed the sack from his shoulder and ran to her. She was lying facedown. A few feet away her hat had been stomped into the dirt and snow.

His heart pounding with fear, Cooper knelt over her and gently touched the back of her head. "Emily! My God, are you all right?"

Groaning, she tried to lever herself off the frozen ground. Her lungs were on fire and her head whirled like a kaleidoscope.

"I think...I..."

Carefully Cooper eased her onto her back, then cradled her head in the crook of his arm. "Try to breathe a little," he instructed. "It'll come back to you."

Her shocked lungs finally managed to draw in more oxygen. As they did, her scrambled senses began to settle back into place. She glanced at the motley herd of cattle milling around them, then up at Cooper's face.

"What happened?"

Gently he brushed the tangled blond hair away from her face. "A steer hit you from behind and knocked you down. How do you feel now? Do you think you're okay? Does anything feel broken?"

Broken? Oh dear Lord, the baby! What had the fall done to it?

What little bit of color that had been returning to Emily's face instantly vanished. "I don't know!" she said in a panicked rush.

He frowned. "What do you mean, you don't know? Can't you tell me whether you're hurting or not?"

"I'm not hurting."

He looked relieved. "Then do you want to try to stand up now?"

She shook her head and tears suddenly collected in her eyes. The baby was everything to her. She couldn't lose it now! "I'm afraid," she whispered.

"Emily, you're not making sense. What are you afraid of? I'll keep the cattle away."

Shaking her head, she bit her lip and glanced away from him. She had to tell him. She couldn't keep her condition from him now. God help her, she might need medical attention. "I'm afraid—for my baby."

He stared at her in stunned disbelief. "Baby? My Lord, are you telling me you're pregnant?"

Slowly she turned her head until her blue eyes were gazing straight into his. "Yes."

His face like granite, Cooper silently lifted her in his arms and carried her to the truck.

"Emily, the best thing you can do now is go home, relax and try not to worry. The results of the ultrasound tell me your baby's heart is beating normally and everything appears to be intact."

Clutching the paper gown against her, Emily looked worriedly up at Dr. Bellamy. The physician was in his seventies, completely white headed and possessed a kindly face, which could normally put the most harried hypochondriac at ease. He'd been her aunt Justine's boss for nearly twenty-five years and during that time he'd delivered her daughter, Caroline, and Emily's younger brother, Ethan. He'd also delivered her aunt Chloe's daughter, Ivy.

"Does that mean the fall didn't hurt the baby?"

Smiling, he gently patted her shoulder. "That's exactly what I'm saying."

With everything inside her, Emily prayed he was right. To have a child of her own was what she'd dreamed and longed for down through the years. If something happened now she didn't know if she could go on.

She tried to relax and swallow the lump of fear in her throat. "But I fell so hard the wind was knocked from me. I can't believe it didn't hurt something."

Seeing her need for extra reassurance, Dr. Bellamy shook his head. "Emily, even though we doctors have all sorts of new technology and knowledge at our fingertips, there's still a lot of things we'll never know. Especially when it comes to pregnancies. A fall on a feather bed can cause some women to miscarry, while others are unaffected by car wrecks and falls from high places. Just be grateful that you appear to be in the latter category."

"But I've miscarried before," she countered in a voice hushed with fear. "Doesn't that mean—"

The doctor folded his arms across his chest and made a tsking noise with his tongue. "It simply means something was wrong with that particular pregnancy," the doctor interrupted her worried argument. "It doesn't mean anything will be wrong with this one."

Walking over to a cabinet counter, he picked up her file. "Now get dressed and go home. Unless something unexpected comes up, which I very much doubt, I'll see you at your next regular checkup."

Emily nodded that she would obey, then thanked him as he went out the examining room door.

Once she was dressed, she found Cooper in the waiting room. From the stoic look on his face it was impossible for Emily to tell what he'd been thinking, however, the moment he spotted her he rose and walked to meet her.

"I'm ready to go home," she told him.

"What did the doctor say?"

Emily figured his question was more perfunctory than anything. From the moment she'd told him about her pregnancy, she'd felt him pulling away, distancing himself from her. She didn't really understand why. Unless it was because he thought she'd cheated Kenneth out of having a child by waiting so late in life to have one. As if she'd had any control over the matter, she thought bitterly.

"He said to go home and relax. He thinks I'm going to be fine."

His expression didn't alter. "Thinks? He doesn't know?"

"Well, he feels pretty certain the both of us are going to be okay. But of course doctors can't always be a hundred percent sure. Especially where pregnancies are concerned."

She walked over to a hall tree and took down her coat. Once she'd pulled it on and buttoned it, she walked back to him. "We can go now. There's nothing else I need to do here at the clinic."

"It's all right for you to walk?"

"I can do anything I want except lift heavy objects."

As if that answered his question completely, she turned and started out of the clinic. Cooper followed and after she'd climbed onto the bench seat in his pickup, he took his place behind the wheel.

From the corner of her eye, Emily watched him start the engine and back out of the parking slot. It had snowed here in Ruidoso, too, but the streets were slushy from the heavier traffic and didn't pose a problem for travelers.

On the drive in from the Diamond D, Cooper had spoken little more than ten words. A few about the weather and even less about how she felt. Now that they were on their way back, she expected even less out of him. Well, that was okay with her, she thought. She didn't want to talk to him about her baby. She didn't want to talk to him about anything. The time for that had passed a long time ago. Like when she'd asked him to stay on the Diamond D, instead of leaving her and heading out to parts unknown.

Cooper was already out of Ruidoso and halfway to Hondo before he realized he'd been so deep in thought he'd not spoken to Emily since the two of them left the clinic.

She probably thought he was angry with her. And maybe he was a little. He didn't know. He was still finding it hard to accept the fact that Emily was pregnant. He didn't want to believe it. Though he couldn't understand why. Emily didn't belong to him. She never had.

"Did my brother know you were pregnant?"

Blurted out of the blue, his question put a look of shocked dismay on Emily's face. "Of course he knew," she answered.

His eyes remained on the highway ahead. "I thought maybe you'd just learned about your condition in the past few days. You look like skin and bones."

Ignoring the part about her appearance, she said, "I'm three and a half months along."

Surprised, he began to do swift calculations in his head. She'd be having the baby in five and a half months! Soon she'd become encumbered by her condition. What had she been thinking when she'd told him she could handle taking care of the ranch? Did she hate him so much she'd tell him anything just to get rid of him?

"I suppose Kenneth was excited about becoming a father?"

Not for anything did she want Cooper to know how opposed Kenneth was to this pregnancy. Glancing away from him, she said, "I guess you could say he was more surprised than anything."

A few moments passed in silence. Glancing at him from beneath her lashes, she saw he was frowning.

"He did want the child, didn't he?"

Emily sighed. She wished Cooper would let it all drop. Kenneth was gone. He'd never be a father to the child she was carrying. So why did it matter to him? she wondered.

"I think deep down he wanted a child. But things had gotten so...well, our financial situation wasn't ready for a surprise pregnancy."

"The pregnancy wasn't planned?"

Planned wasn't exactly the right word for it, Emily thought. True, she hadn't been using birth control, but after years of trying to get pregnant and failing, she hadn't seen any need for prevention. When Dr. Bellamy had given her the news she was expecting, she'd been shocked and ecstatic. Kenneth had simply been stunned.

She frowned at him. "Do you really think that's any of your business?"

Cooper supposed it wasn't. But he couldn't explain how she'd been in his heart all these years. He couldn't tell her how even though he'd been gone, he'd thought and wondered and wanted to know everything about her.

"Forget it," he muttered. "You don't have to tell me anything. I'm just a little taken aback that Kenneth wasn't thrilled about becoming a father after all this time."

Tears were suddenly biting her throat. She tried to tell herself it was because Kenneth hadn't really wanted this child. But she knew in her heart the tears were for the baby she'd lost ten years ago, the baby Cooper had never known about.

"Kenneth had a lot of worries," she murmured. "My being pregnant had added to the list."

"So he never really wanted children?"

Emily's gaze dropped to her lap. She was still dressed in her old work clothes. Dried mud from where she'd fallen still clung to the front of her jeans. She knew she looked horrible and for the first time in a long time, she was ashamed of her appearance.

"At first Kenneth wanted a child. But I...we were never able to conceive. After a few years he gave up on the notion."

"But you never did."

For years Emily had desperately wanted a child to nourish and love and to have that child love and need her in return. And in all that time she'd never completely given up hope that God would give her a baby. She hadn't expected Cooper to pick up on those feelings. The fact that he had left a bittersweet ache in her heart.

"No. I never gave up."

The remainder of the trip was made in silence. Emily was relieved when the ranch finally came into view. The day had been traumatic for her in more ways than one. Now she simply wanted to lie down and try to gather her tangled emotions back together.

With Emily resting in her bedroom, Cooper was at a loss as to what to do next. As he wandered restlessly around the living room, he considered all the things he should be doing and those he wanted to do.

It was unusual for him to have free time on his hands. Even just a half a day. Normally he was on the road driving from one town and one state to the next.

Rodeo had been good to him. He couldn't deny that. But it had also stolen many things from him. A home, a family, the simple joy of watching the sun rise and set in the same place.

But then he hadn't planned on making the sport his life for ten years. Nor had he planned on Emily marrying Kenneth a few short months after he'd left, either. But she had. And because of her, Cooper had lived the life of a nomad ever since.

With a weary sigh, he walked over to the fireplace and stacked several logs on the dying embers. He didn't know what Kenneth would think about him being here now and a part of him didn't care. Except for her parents, Emily was alone and pregnant and very nearly bankrupt. She obviously didn't want him here. But in all good conscience, he couldn't leave her now.

A few hours later the sky was growing dusky dark when Cooper looked up from his hammering to see Emily approaching the barn where he was working on the roof. Though it had quit snowing several hours ago, the wind was bitterly cold. He figured she didn't need to be out in the weather. However, it was quickly becoming apparent to him that Emily was still as strong minded as she used to be. She wouldn't take kindly to his ordering her around. Even if the order had concern for her welfare behind it.

"What are you doing down here?" he asked. "I've already fed the horses."

She tilted her head back and gazed up at his lofty perch. "I figured as much. I came down to tell you supper was ready."

It didn't make sense, Cooper thought, as he looked down at her. Everything she said pointed to the fact that she hated him. Yet she'd walked all the way out here in the freezing cold just to tell him it was time to eat.

Jamming the hammer and nails into his coat pocket, he slid down the corrugated iron until he reached the ladder propped against the side of the building. Before he put his boot on the first rung, Emily grabbed the bottom of the ladder to steady it as he climbed down.

Once he was standing on the ground, he thanked her for her thoughtfulness and for a moment he believed he saw a blush on her cheeks. But night was quickly falling, sending shadows playing across her hat and face.

"What were you doing up there?" she asked as the two of them headed across the barren ranch yard, toward the back of the house. "I didn't think there was any more extra corrugated iron in the barn."

"I wasn't replacing it, just nailing it down where the edges had torn loose. Hopefully it will last for a while. Tomorrow, I'll drive into Ruidoso and buy some supplies. Maybe you can give me some sort of idea what else is needed around here and we'll make a list."

His words should have comforted her, Emily supposed. What normal woman, pregnant at that, wouldn't want a strong man around to help her? But Cooper wasn't just any man. He made her think and hurt. Just looking at him brought her close to tears. She couldn't take that sort of mental torture day after day. She had the baby to think about now!

"I thought you were leaving," she said flatly.

The ground was rough and rocky between the barn and the house. Several times Cooper caught himself wanting to reach for her arm to steady her. But he didn't. When he'd touched her earlier today at the feed grounds, he'd sensed an undercurrent of sorts. If there was a dormant fire still simmering between them, he definitely didn't want to wake it up. One physical relationship with her had more than taught him a lesson.

"There's no way in hell I'll leave now."

"Why?"

He opened the door and motioned her inside. "Get in the house."

After their coats were off, Emily placed dishes of food on the table while Cooper tried to answer her question.

"It should be obvious to you," he said patiently. "I can't leave you now."

Slowly Emily turned away from the cookstove. Her eyes pinned him with a look of angry disbelief. It was incredible that he was saying this to her now. Ten years too late! She wanted to yell and curse at him, pound her fist against his chest until there was no pain, no tears left inside her.

"Get this straight, Cooper Dunn, I am no concern of yours. You might own part of this ranch, but you don't own me. You never did and you never will!"

Her outburst should have infuriated Cooper, but if anything it worried and puzzled him. The bitter fury in her eyes was so deep and strong he felt physically struck by it.

"Emily—" Compelled by the need to calm her, he crossed the room and lay his hand on her shoulder. She was outwardly trembling. "Emily—" he began again, his voice husky with concern. "What's wrong? You're so upset you're going to make yourself sick."

The touch of his hand snapped her back to the moment and she realized she had to draw herself together and fast. The last thing she wanted to do was let Cooper know how much he'd hurt her. Even worse, how very much she'd loved him.

She drew in a long breath and let it out slowly. "I'm okay. I'm—" Her gaze dropped to the toes of his boots. "My nerves are frayed, Cooper. Every little thing sets me off. I didn't mean to lay into you so harshly. I just—want you to understand that my being pregnant has nothing to do with you."

Her face was so pale and drawn. He wanted to smooth his fingers over her cheeks until her skin bloomed rosy and full of life again. "The child is my niece or nephew."

"That's true. But that doesn't mean you have to alter your life."

His hand unconsciously began to knead her shoulder. "Maybe I shouldn't remind you of this, but you know my mother died giving birth to me."

"Cooper—"

"She was headstrong just like you," he went on before Emily could stop him. "When she came down with a fever Dad wanted to take her to the hospital, but she insisted a good night's sleep was all she needed. She went into early labor. Coupled with the fever, it was too much strain on her heart. She died before she ever had the chance to hold me in her arms."

Tears blurred Emily's eyes. She squeezed them tightly shut and swallowed several times. "It won't be like that for me, Cooper. I'll take care of myself. You see that I went straight to the clinic today after my fall."

"Yes. But you need someone here to look after you."

She wiped her eyes and looked up at him. The gentle regard on his face both touched and angered her. If only he'd shown her as much ten years ago. If only he'd wanted to stay and take care of her then when she'd needed and wanted him so badly. But he hadn't known she was pregnant with his child. And neither had she, until he'd already been gone for two months. He shouldn't be blamed for something he hadn't known about. But God forgive her, she did blame him. She couldn't help herself.

"If need be, my mother can stay with me."

One corner of his mouth crooked upward. "Do you think that's fair to her?"

Ruffled again, she stared into his clear gray eyes. "I'm her daughter. She loves me and would do anything for me."

"I'm sure of it. But as I remember, your mother and father were a very close couple and spent lots of time together. Or has that changed now that they're a little older?"

Seeing what he was getting at, she shook her head. "No. It hasn't changed. And if you're trying to make me feel like a burden, you're doing a good job."

"I'm not trying to make you feel like a burden. I'm trying to make you see you need someone here with you."

Her mouth fell open and she laughed harshly. "And you think you're that someone? Get real, Cooper. You're not a man who could stay in one place for more than a week, much less look after a pregnant woman."

"How do you know?"

At some point in the last few minutes, she'd become aware of his hand moving gently against her shoulder. Now it was beginning to burn through her knit top like a red-hot branding iron.

Desperate to halt her runaway senses, she shrugged out of his grasp and reached for a basket of warm taco shells.

"Have you ever lived with a woman, Cooper?"

Caught completely off guard by her question, he watched her go over to the dining table and take a seat at one of the place settings.

"What does that have to do with anything?" he asked crossly.

She glanced at him, then set about filling her plate. "Maybe nothing. Maybe I'm just curious."

Snorting, he joined her at the table and took his own place at an angle to her right. "I seriously doubt you've had one curious moment over me since I left here."

She'd had a million curious moments, but she'd never confess that to him. She'd rather eat nails than have him knowing how much she'd grieved for him after he'd went away.

"What about the woman? Or women, I should say."

He glanced at her sharply, then reached for a taco shell. "I haven't been married or anything, if that's what you're asking."

"I didn't really figure you had," she said bluntly. Years ago, Cooper had made it clear enough to her that he wasn't ready to become a married man. Looking at him now, she could see he hadn't changed. He still had that tough, loner, I'm-my-own-man look about him.

A dull flush spread over his face. "I lived with a woman for a while," he muttered. "Or at least when I was between rodeos."

Her brows arched. "You didn't want to marry her?"

He shook his head and Emily found her gaze wandering over his thick dark hair, cool gray eyes and sensual mouth. Most women would find him more than attractive. He'd probably never had to look very hard for female companionship whenever he'd felt in the mood for it. But had he ever been in love? Had he ever needed someone as much as she had once needed him?

"She had a young son by a former marriage," he went on. "The kid hated the very sight of me."

"And whose fault was that? Did you try to get along with him?"

Cooper grimaced as he stuffed the corn shell full of meat and fresh vegetables. "As best I could. He didn't want to share his mother with me. And I guess I'm too much like my old man. I'm just not that good at fathering."

Not bothering to hide her surprise, she studied his face. "Why do you say that? Kenneth always spoke lovingly of his father."

He shrugged as though the subject meant little to him, but somehow Emily knew otherwise.

"I loved William, too," he told her. "But he wasn't the best of fathers. Not in my eyes. Of course, things were different for Kenneth."

"What do you mean things were different?"

His features stiffened. "Ask anyone who knew my old man, Emily. Kenneth was his chosen one. He could do no wrong. I could never do anything right. I've told you this before. But I guess you've pretty much forgotten anything I ever said."

Where Cooper was concerned, she hadn't forgotten anything. Emily did remember him calling himself the second best son. At the time she'd thought he'd only meant it in terms of his ranching responsibilities, or more rightly, his lack of them.

"I remember. But that was all about the ranch. I'm sure your father loved you just as much."

He snorted. "Not hardly. I knew each time William looked at me he couldn't help but think about the wife he lost. But what the hell, I learned to live with it. I just didn't learn anything about fathering from him."

In spite of all the pain this man had caused her, she felt her heart softening, wishing for his sake that his childhood had been better. Reaching for her milk glass, she asked, "What about the woman? You didn't love her enough to try to stay or make it work with her child?"

He shook his head. "She wanted me to be a family man. You know that isn't me."

Yes, she had known it. But Emily had believed and hoped he might love her enough to change, to want to be a family man just for her. What a horrid mistake that had been.

"A person isn't necessarily born knowing how to be a parent or a spouse. You have to learn by doing," she told him.

"And what if a person does it all wrong?"

She shrugged. "No one is perfect. You learn from your mistakes and try to do better."

Leaning back in his chair, he studied her as he chewed a bite of taco. "Sometimes the damage is already done and you can't go on and do better."

Was he talking about him and her? No. He couldn't be. As far as he was concerned leaving her hadn't been a mistake. "Then you pick up the pieces and go on as best you can." Just as she'd had to do years ago, she thought. And just as she was doing now.

Cooper's eyes drifted away from her. "Well, I think I'd rather be alone. I don't want to be responsible for another person's happiness. Especially a kid's."

Her nostrils flared as she tried to hold on to her anger. "Then why don't you go on and be alone somewhere else and let me handle my own business?"

Because she was his business, Cooper thought with dawning realization. When he'd come to that conclusion, he didn't know. He only knew he couldn't go on his merry way while she stayed here on the Diamond D, pregnant and alone.

He looked back at her and wondered about the sudden pain in his heart. "I will. When the time is right."

# Chapter Four

"Daddy, he's beautiful!" Emily exclaimed as she watched the big Appaloosa gelding trot around the round metal pen. "Where did you find him?"

Smiling at the pleasure on his daughter's face, Harlan Hamilton wrapped his arm around her shoulder. "At the horse sale in Clovis. What do you think about him?"

She grinned impishly up at him. "He looks just like my old App, Apache. How much did you have to give for him?"

Harlan laughed. "Now why would I tell you? You don't let someone know how much you spent on their gift."

Her mouth fell open. "Gift? Oh, no. You're not going to give me that horse."

Her father laughed again. "Then who am I going to give him to?"

"Well, I—I don't know," she stammered. "Keep him for yourself."

"I don't even like Appaloosas. You do. Besides, another horse is the last thing your mother and I need. We probably have thirty head now."

She looked up at her father, who was still a handsome, virile man even though he was nearing sixty. He and Rose had worked hard to make the Flying H the beautiful ranch it was today. No easy feat considering they'd married during a devastating drought and family turmoil. But the two of them had persevered through those trials and many more problems down through the years. Now the ranch was beautiful and solvent and blessed with all the livestock it needed.

Her parents' hard work and success had always been an inspiration to Emily. If they could do it, then so could she and Kenneth. But down through the years, Emily had learned a couple needed more than hard work and determination to make it through the troubles and heartaches life dishes out. They needed undying, unconditional love. And God help her, she just hadn't felt that sort of love for Kenneth.

She'd had a deep affection for him and she'd respected him. But she should have never married him. It had taken Emily only a few short weeks to realize she'd made a mistake in letting Kenneth talk her into becoming his wife. But at the time he'd proposed, she was still raw from Cooper's rejection, not to mention still grieving over the miscarriage she'd told no one, not even her parents, about. She'd felt alone and unloved and Kenneth's attention had been a balm to her broken heart. But she hadn't loved him. Try as she might, she'd never been able to make herself feel for him the way she'd felt about Cooper.

"Would you like for me to saddle him for you, honey?"

Her father's question pulled her out of her deep thoughts. She smiled up at him and shook her head. "It's only been a little over a week since I took that fall at the feed grounds. I'd better wait about doing any riding."

He patted her shoulder. "You're going to be fine, sweetheart. The only trouble you're going to have is keeping your mother away from that baby once it gets here."

She hugged his waist and briefly pressed her cheek against his broad chest. "Thank you for the horse, Daddy. Will you bring him over to the ranch for me?"

"Today, if you like."

Rising on tiptoe, she kissed his cheek. "Thanks, Daddy. I think I'll go up to the house now and see Mom for a few minutes before I go home."

Nodding, he tweaked her cheek. "Okay. I'll see you later. And Emily," he added as she started walking away, "it's good to see you smile again."

She hadn't realized she'd smiled. She hadn't even known she could. But she was glad she'd made her father happy. He was the one man who'd always loved her, who would always love her.

At the house she found her mother in the kitchen baking pumpkin bread. The room was warm and so full of potted plants it looked more like a hothouse than a ranch kitchen.

"Darling! I didn't know you'd driven up. Does your daddy know you're here?"

She wiped her floured hands on a dish towel and hurried over to kiss Emily's cheek. "You look much better since I last saw you! There's color in your cheeks and you look like you've been eating, thank God."

Emily hugged her mother, then took a seat on a nearby bar stool. "I've been trying to eat all I can."

"That's wonderful to hear. And it's so nice to see you dressed up and wearing makeup. I hope this is a sign your spirits are lifting."

Emily glanced down at her black jeans and cranberry colored sweater. She wasn't dressed up by any means, but compared to the way she had been going around, it probably looked that way to her mother. But since the day of her fall and Cooper's not so kind remarks about her appearance, she'd made a point of paying closer attention to her hair and skin and clothes.

"Actually my spirits are much better. And to answer

your earlier question, I've already seen Daddy. Why didn't you tell me about the horse?''

Rose went back to stirring her bowl of batter. "Because it was his surprise. I didn't want to spoil his fun."

"Well, he shouldn't have spent the money."

"He wanted to. Besides, you need a good horse. Those you have on the Diamond D aren't the best in the world."

Emily gave her mother a wry smile. "They can't all be like your beloved Pie."

"I guess I am spoiled by him," Rose said with obvious fondness.

"Not to mention attached. You know horses can't live forever, Mom."

Rose shrugged and smiled. "No. But Pie's doing a good job of it. He's twenty-five and still going strong. The vet says if I continue to take good care of him he'll probably last ten more."

"Well, there's no doubt he'll get good care around here."

Rose poured the batter into a row of tin loaf pans, then placed them in the oven. Once she was finished, she took two mugs down from the cabinet and poured them full of coffee.

"It's decaffeinated," she assured Emily as she took a stool beside her.

With a murmur of appreciation, Emily sipped the warm brew. "It's so wonderful not to be sickened by the smell of coffee. Knock on wood, I believe my nausea has finally passed once and for all."

"That's good to hear. You've had enough to deal with these days." Crossing her legs, Rose looked at her thoughtfully. "So tell me what's been happening. Is Cooper still staying with you?"

Emily sighed. She really wasn't in the mood to discuss Cooper with her mother. He was like a raw spot. Every time she thought about him she flinched with pain. "He's gone to Ruidoso today to check about getting liquid feed for the cattle.''

Rose nodded with approval. ''That's good. You never did have enough grazing land. The licks will help.''

Emily knew her mother was right. The Diamond D cattle needed all the nourishment they could get, but it irked her to have Cooper supplying it.

Gazing into her coffee cup, she said, ''Daddy didn't ask me anything about Cooper. You did tell him he was back on the Diamond D, didn't you?''

''Yes, I told him. I expect he didn't mention Cooper because he figures the guy is just passing through and his being here isn't going to make any difference one way or the other.''

Emily wished she could think in those terms. ''I hope he's right. I hope Cooper is just passing through, but he keeps telling me otherwise.''

''Do you think he really means to stay?''

Closing her eyes, Emily drew in a long breath, then let it out slowly. ''Deep down I think this is just a passing thing with Cooper. I think the luster will wear off soon and he'll decide to hit the road again. Personally I can't wait.''

''Why? Has he been—forward with you?''

Opening her eyes, Emily looked at her mother. ''In what way?''

''In any way.''

Emily grimaced. ''Why do you ask something like that?''

Rose gave her daughter a gentle smile. ''Darling, the man was attracted to you at one time.''

Cooper had been attracted to her, Emily silently agreed. But the attraction had only been a physical thing, and certainly nothing strong enough to keep him here in New Mexico. ''Oh, Mother, that was so long ago. It doesn't mean anything now.''

"Maybe not to you. But Cooper might not have forgotten."

"Mother! That's...well, I can't believe you of all people could even think such a thing!"

Rose actually laughed, surprising Emily even more.

"It isn't really such a shocking thing," Rose insisted. "You're still a young, beautiful woman. And for some reason Cooper has never married."

"Not because of me!"

"How do you know? Did you ask him?"

Emily gasped at her mother's question. "Of course not! I mean—well, I did ask him if he'd married. But that was...only because I was curious. Any self-respecting man would know I'm still grieving over my husband."

Sighing, Rose took another drink of coffee. "Are you grieving, honey?"

Emily stared at her mother as if the older woman had suddenly lost all her senses and morality. "Mother! What has come over you? Do you think I wanted Kenneth to die?"

Seeing how offended her daughter was becoming, Rose slid from the stool and curled her arm around Emily's shoulder. "Darling, calm down. I'm not thinking anything of the sort. But I am going to speak frankly to you. Because I think it's what you need now."

Emily went very still as she looked into her mother's lovely face. "Talk to me frankly? About what?"

"You. I realize down through the years I never really questioned you about your marriage to Kenneth."

"No. You've never been an interfering parent."

Rose shook her head. "I've tried not to be. But actually, I didn't have to ask about your marriage. I knew you weren't happy. At least, not happy the way your father and I are."

Emily's gaze dropped to her lap. "Not every couple is as blessed as you and Daddy."

Rose smiled softly. "No. Not every couple. And I realize Kenneth's death was a dreadful shock to you. I know you would have given anything for the accident to have never happened. But that's not the same as the deep devastation a woman feels when she loses her soul mate—"

"But Kenneth—"

"Wasn't your soul mate," Rose finished before Emily could.

Emily opened her mouth to further protest, but then her shoulders sagged with resignation. Dropping her head, she asked, "Are you trying to make me feel guiltier than I already do?"

Rose took the mug from Emily's hand. After placing it on the bar, she pressed her daughter's hands between her own. "Now we have finally reached the real issue I wanted to speak to you about."

Emily stared at her blankly.

"For years now I've seen you carrying around a heavy blanket of guilt. It's time you threw it away."

"Guilt? I don't—"

Shaking her head, Rose smiled and cupped her daughter's face in her hands. "Emily, do you remember when your father and I first met? You were thirteen and a little bit wary of me. Until you found out that, like you, I had lost my mother, too."

Emily nodded. "That was twenty-three years ago, but I remember it like yesterday." She and her father had moved here from east Texas when Emily had been seven and her birth mother had died. Up until Rose had come into their life, she'd had little female companionship.

"You said we were kindred spirits then," Rose said. "And I think we still are. That's why I know how you've been feeling. You've always believed you let Kenneth down. That you didn't love him enough. That it was your fault you couldn't get pregnant. And now I think you even feel guilty about his accident. As though you caused it in some way.''

Emily felt a giant rubber band inside her snap with relief. Still, she murmured, ''Like Cooper said, I shouldn't have let him get on that horse. But I've—''

''Emily—''

Emily held up a hand to ward off her mother's protest. ''I've decided that whatever I was to Kenneth, I wasn't his keeper. I couldn't watch him every moment as though he were an irresponsible child.''

Rose patted her daughter's hand, then resumed her seat on the bar stool. ''Now you're talking like a sensible woman.''

''I don't know if I'm sensible or not. But I damn well don't intend to let Cooper take me down. Not over Kenneth's death. Not over anything.''

Her expression thoughtful again, Rose said, ''You know, when I was around Cooper I always liked him. I just didn't approve of the way he handled things with you. Is he anything like he used to be?''

Her face grim, Emily said, ''Exactly. And I wish he was gone. I wish I never had to see his face again.''

''Well, I'm beginning to think the man ought to hang around. This is the most spunk I've seen in you in years.''

Emily let out a harsh laugh. ''This isn't spunk you're seeing, Mother. It's fury.''

''Whatever it is, it's better than the sight of your chin drooping down to your knees.''

''Mom, I really think I should start coming over here and checking on you more often. You're not acting like yourself.''

With a little knowing smile, Rose left her seat and went to check on the baking pumpkin bread. ''Maybe you're just starting to see things you haven't seen in a long time, honey.''

"I don't know why your dad bought you a horse," Cooper said later that same day as he watched Emily stroke the Appaloosa's nose. "There's probably a hundred other things around here you needed more."

Emily turned to look at him as he walked up to the outside of the wooden corral. "Maybe Daddy gave me the horse because he wanted to give me something I'd like. Rather than something I necessarily needed."

Cooper pushed his gray hat to the back of his head and propped his forearms over the top rail of the pen. "I guess things haven't changed as much as I thought around here."

She walked away from the horse, whose registered name was Native Moon, and over to where Cooper was resting casually against the fence. It was a warm, sunny afternoon. One of those precious last few she expected them to have before winter set in permanently. The sky was brilliant azure and the air carried the fresh biting scent of sage and juniper. It was a day to enjoy and Emily realized for the most part she had enjoyed it. In spite of Cooper Dunn.

"What do you mean by that?" she asked him, while noticing he, too, had shed his jacket and rolled the sleeves of his denim shirt back on his forearms.

"That your daddy still spoils you."

Emily wasn't going to allow his remark to anger her. It wasn't worth ruining the day over. "That's his right."

Smiling because she didn't bother to deny it, he said, "I guess that's true. But it does make me wonder why he hasn't stepped in to help you with things here on the ranch before now. I wouldn't have thought Harlan Hamilton would have allowed his daughter to live on a place like the Diamond D."

A few days ago Emily would have been insulted by his remarks. But now she could only look at him and wonder and try to imagine what it must have been like growing up on this place and feeling as though he was nothing more than a shadow of his older brother. He'd obviously never been spoiled by William Dunn in any shape or fashion. It was probably hard for him to understand that Harlan still took pleasure in giving his daughter gifts, even though she was thirty-six years old.

"My father never believed in giving me handouts. Not that I would have taken them anyway. And after I married Kenneth he didn't butt into our business. If I ask him for help, he's always glad to oblige. But sink or swim, I'd rather make it on my own."

Considering the present condition of the Diamond D, Cooper thought that a pretty tall rather. If he hadn't come home, how had she planned on surviving? It didn't sound as though she'd expected financial help from her parents.

"Did Kenneth have a life insurance policy?"

She frowned at him. "Yes. Why?"

"Just curious," he said, then tugged his hat down on his forehead.

"Don't worry. I'm going to put all the money back into the ranch. I wasn't planning on fluffing it off on designer clothes and jewelry," she said dryly.

"I wish you would spend it on yourself," he said earnestly.

Casting him a doubtful look, she said, "Sure you do."

Her sarcasm stung him. "Do you think I'm that selfish?"

Ten years ago she'd thought he was the most selfish man on earth. While his leg had been mending, he'd given her the impression she, and only she, was all that mattered to him. But as soon as the doctor had given him his walking papers, he'd started packing. Oh, he'd tried to say he was leaving for her, to come back with enough money to buy them a ranch of their own.

But Emily hadn't wanted money or another ranch and she'd told him so. The only thing she'd wanted or needed was for them to be together. But he'd turned a deaf ear to her and left in spite of her pleadings. Selfish? The word didn't begin to describe what she'd thought of him.

"I refuse to answer on the grounds it might incriminate me."

He frowned at her. "Whatever you might think about me, I don't want Kenneth's money. I didn't even think I wanted my part of this ranch...until the other day when I saw it again."

"Now *that* I do believe."

"And you think it strange I never really tried to make the most of my part of the Diamond D, don't you?" he asked.

His expression had grown soft as if seeing her face in the sun pleased him and Emily found it very hard to hold his gaze, to accept the warm gentleness in his eyes.

She nodded. "I could never understand you wanting some other ranch. This place is your birthright."

"I shouldn't have a birthright," he said flatly. "My birth caused my mother's death."

She hated hearing him say such a horrible thing. He might deserve a guilty conscience for breaking her heart, but he should never feel guilty about his mother's death.

"You don't really believe you caused your mother to die."

He looked away from her and out over the rolling desert hills and distant barren mountains. "My father believed it."

"Apparently not. He left you half the ranch in his will."

"Yeah, but he made it clear who he wanted running it." He looked back at her. "This place has always belonged to someone else. Not me. A man likes to have something of his own, Emily. If you can understand that, maybe you could forgive me for leaving all those years ago."

Since he'd arrived on the ranch a little over a week and a half ago, he'd never once talked about that time in their lives. And Emily had decided there was no point in bringing it up. She'd already said enough to make it clear to him how she felt about his long-term absence. As for forgiving him, she couldn't believe her forgiveness mattered to him one way or the other.

"Oh, I understand perfectly why you left, Cooper."

The sarcasm in her voice told him she hadn't been listening to a word he'd said. Not back then. And not now.

But maybe that was for the best, he thought, as he pushed himself away from the fence. That part of their life was over. He needed to coexist with her simply as his sister-in-law and nothing more.

Tugging his hat back down on his forehead, he said, "The App is a beauty. I hope you enjoy him."

He turned and walked away. Her mouth open, Emily stared after him. What was he doing? How could he bring up such a raw subject, then leave as if they'd been discussing no more than the weather?

Color burning high on her cheeks, she let herself out of the corral and headed toward the barn. She caught up to him in the tack room. He was clutching a fistful of bridles and bits and from the surprised look on his face, she knew he hadn't been expecting her to follow him.

"What?" he blurted. "Is something wrong?"

She marched up to within an inch of him and stared up at his shadowed face. "Yes. Something is wrong. Why did you walk away just now?"

His brows lifted innocently. "Because I have work I want to get finished before dark."

She stopped herself just short of snorting. "Don't act innocent with me, Cooper. You can't just open a can of worms then walk off like that."

His eyes narrowed on her face and before Emily knew it, her thoughts were wandering, straying back to those days when he'd been her lover. He'd made her feel so special, so loved. Just looking at him had taken her breath away. And it very nearly did now. As her eyes clung to the chiseled line of his lips, she was certain the tack room had grown smaller and darker.

"Look, Emily, I don't even know why I said what I did I don't expect you to give me a long speech about how you understand and forgive me. I don't even need that from you, so forget I ever said anything."

He didn't need forgiveness from her. So far that hurt more than anything he'd said. "If that's the way you feel. why did you mention it at all?"

Turning away from her, Cooper stared into a dark corner of the room while his fingers absently rubbed a frayed piece of leather. "I don't know. Just a moment of foolish sentimentality, I guess. Maybe it had something to do with you dad giving you the App. It made me think of another time—before I ever met you."

Curiosity swiftly replaced Emily's anger. "What were you remembering?"

"Nothing really. Just another horse. I'd spotted him over in Roswell and was making plans to buy him when Dad stepped in and bought him for Kenneth instead."

"Oh—" The word escaped her as a tiny gasp and he turned back to her, a twisted smile on his face.

"Childish of me, huh? To still remember something so trivial?"

Trivial? If her father had done something like that to her, she was certain she would never forget it. "How could he have done something so—so hurtful?"

He let out a harsh laugh. "William didn't view that as hurtful."

"What about Kenneth? Surely he knew the horse should have been yours!"

Cooper shrugged as though the incident was hardly worth mentioning. "He told me he tried to persuade the old man to give the horse to me. But I'm not so sure he was being honest. A few weeks later, Dad let it slip about Kenneth begging him for the horse. And William never could tell his favorite son no."

Emily shook her head. "But that's awful, Cooper! I can't

believe Kenneth would do such an underhanded thing to you! When I met the two of you, it appeared you and your brother got along very well.''

He moved away from her and a swirl of mixed emotions washed through Emily as she watched him take another handful of bridles from a nail on the wall.

''We weren't always the best of buddies. But we didn't fight. When we were growing up Kenneth always used to tell me what a raw deal he thought Dad was giving me. Funny thing, though, he never would stand up to Dad for me. I've wondered about that a lot down through the years. I guess it didn't bother Kenneth to see me as the whipping boy so long as he stayed in good graces with the old man.''

Emily didn't know what to make of all he'd told her. She couldn't imagine any man being so cruel to his brother. But then she knew Kenneth hadn't been without a mean, moody streak. The last year of their marriage had been so difficult, she'd often wondered how she could go on. Still, her husband had always left her with the impression that he loved Cooper. Had she been wrong?

''Back then, didn't you have some sort of responsibility on the ranch? If Kenneth took care of the cattle, what did you do?''

Cooper grimaced. ''Not much in those days. By then I didn't give a damn about the place. I'd already been cut out.''

One by one, Cooper began to inspect the bridles and hackamores. The ones that needed mending he tossed on a nearby hay bale, the others he hung back on the nail. As Emily stood to the side, watching him, it came to her that even though she'd loved this man, she hadn't really known him. Oh, she'd known what it was like to kiss him, talk and laugh with him, even make love to him. But never had she gotten a real glimpse of the man underneath. Maybe he hadn't wanted her to.

''You think I'm like your father, don't you?'' she asked,

the mere idea sickening her. "You believe I chose Kenneth over you, that I think you don't belong here."

He stared at the dry, brittle leather in his hands. "You said it. I didn't."

She couldn't think of a single word she could say or one thing she could do to make him see she hadn't felt that way. Nor did she understand why it even mattered to her. He'd hurt her. But had she hurt him, too? Is that what he'd been trying to tell her?

"Cooper...I always felt like you should have a part of this ranch. Until I believed you didn't want it."

He tossed the remaining bridles aside and walked toward her. His eyes were shadowed with anger. Or was it pain? Emily was still trying to figure which when his hands grasped her upper arms.

"And you believed I didn't want you," he said in a deceptively soft voice. "Is that what you're telling me?"

Suddenly her heart was pounding. Not because he had dredged up a past she wanted to forget, but because he was touching her, looking at her as if time had never passed.

"Kenneth loved me. And you didn't. It was that simple." Actually there'd been nothing simple about it. But she needed to make him believe so. The way she was feeling at the moment it wouldn't be safe to pour her heart out to him. She doubted it would ever be safe.

"For a woman who was twenty-five years old back then you were very naive," he said.

Her nostrils flared with anger and anticipation. "Thank you. That's just what I needed to hear."

Before the last word was past her lips, he was giving her shoulders a shake. "You need to hear a lot of things. But right now—" In stunned fascination, Emily watched his face dip down toward hers. "I don't think words could get the message across," he murmured.

"Cooper, don't—"

The rest of her protest was blotted out by the hard line of his lips, the clamp of his arms around her shoulders.

Shock and confusion slammed Emily from all directions, then as the warmth of his mouth plundered hers, it no longer mattered why he was kissing her, only that he was. And that he tasted the same, felt the same! The realization very nearly made her weep with a mixture of joy and regret.

Unknowingly her hands crept up his chest and linked at the back of his neck. Her mouth opened to the erotic search of his lips. This was the Cooper she had loved, she thought, as a blissful sigh swept a shudder through her body. This was the Cooper that had made her so happy.

And so sad. So terribly, terribly sad.

Frantic to end the fusion of their lips, Emily shoved herself away from him. "You haven't changed one little bit," she muttered hoarsely.

His lips twisted wryly. "Shall I take that as a compliment?"

"You're despicable to...to take advantage of me!"

He threw back his head and let loose a harsh laugh. "Maybe I was guilty of that ten years ago. But as you just said, you're not naive anymore. You know what a bastard I am."

Her hands clenched at her sides as her blue eyes bored into his. "There's no reason for you to be deliberately crude!"

"And there's no reason for you to be overdramatic, either. That was just a little kiss. It's not like we made mad passionate love to each other."

Maybe it hadn't felt like it to him, Emily thought. But it sure had to her. "And we're not going to make mad passionate love of any kind, either!"

"No," he agreed. "We're not. But I am a man. Plain and simple. With wants and needs just like any other man. I guess somewhere along the way you forgot that."

Well, if she had, he'd certainly reminded her of it a few

moments ago. Her lips were still burning and she knew the pounding of her heart had filled her face with color.

"I didn't know I needed to make a point of remembering your gender," she retorted, while wishing the sight of him didn't have the power to excite her, to make her want and wish for things that couldn't be.

Cooper watched the rapid rise and fall of her breasts, a scarlet flame licking across her cheeks, and deep inside him he wondered how he could ever stay here now and not love her.

Or had he ever stopped loving her?

# Chapter Five

"Emily, you are coming to the Bar M for Thanksgiving, aren't you?"

As Emily waited for the receptionist to write her an appointment card, she glanced at her aunt Justine. Like her mother, she was a tall beautiful redhead who carried her age incredibly well. Since she worked at the clinic as a nurse, Justine saw her each time she came in for a visit with Dr. Bellamy.

"To be honest, I hadn't really thought that much about Thanksgiving. Mother mentioned it earlier this month. I suppose my parents will be there?"

"Of course they'll be there. And hopefully the rest of the family. Although I'm never certain about Charlie."

Emily's cousin, Charlie, was a Texas Ranger. And though she knew Justine and Roy were very proud of him, she was well aware that they worried about him a great deal, too.

"I guess he never knows until the last minute whether he'll be able to get off work," Emily remarked. "Have you talked with him lately? How's he doing?"

Justine sighed. "My son is working himself to death. But he insists it's what he wants to do."

Emily smiled at her aunt. "Charlie always puts his heart in whatever he does. That's why he's such a good Ranger."

Justine sighed once more, but this time a smile accompanied it. "I know. I just wish he'd put a little more heart into finding a wife."

Emily had always been close to Charlie and she wanted him to be happy. She didn't want him to marry just for the sake of being married. She wanted him to find a woman who would be wonderful to him.

"I'm sure he will one of these days, Aunt Justine. Just let him do it on his own."

Justine nodded with understanding. "Charlie wouldn't let me interfere even if I wanted to. Now what about Thanksgiving? We'll miss you if you're not there."

"Well, I don't know. I..." The Bar M was the Murdock home place. Although Chloe, the youngest of the three sisters actually lived there now, Justine and Rose still considered it their home, too. Most all holidays and family reunions were held there because it had the biggest house and because the old ranch had been a major reason for bringing all three Murdock sisters to their future husbands. It was a family place, through and through. How could she take Cooper there?

"Well, I don't know. I..."

Justine regarded her thoughtfully. "Is Cooper still on the Diamond D with you?"

Other than her mother's opinion and her father's lack of one, Emily didn't have any idea what the rest of her family thought about Cooper being back in Lincoln county and living in the same house with her.

"Yes. He's been...working hard, trying to get the place patched back together."

Justine smiled warmly. "Then you must bring him with you, too. Unless he has—other commitments somewhere."

Emily grimaced. ''If you mean a family, Cooper doesn't have any.''

''Oh, how sad.'' She smiled again and patted Emily's shoulder. ''That's all the more reason you should bring him along.''

Emily opened her mouth to tell Justine she didn't think Cooper was the family holidaying sort, but her aunt reached for a stack of medical files on the counter and started back down the hallway toward the examining rooms.

''Take care of yourself, honey, and we'll see you later,'' she called back to Emily.

With a sigh Emily took the card from the receptionist and walked to the front entrance of the building. The weather was cold and snowy and Cooper had refused to let her drive into Ruidoso on her own. Earlier, he'd dropped her off at the clinic for her monthly checkup, then went on to take care of some business of his own.

Buttoning her coat, she glanced at her wristwatch. She'd been here for more than an hour. He should be driving up any moment.

Less than five minutes later, she spotted his black pickup pulling into the clinic parking lot. Tossing the hood of her coat over her head, she left the warmth of the building.

Halfway down the sidewalk Cooper met her and she looked up with surprise as he took hold of her arm.

''You might slip on the snow,'' he explained his actions, then added with a frown, ''I don't know why you wore those cowboy boots with slick leather soles.''

''Probably because my snow boots are worn out and these at least keep my feet dry.''

In the past month and a half since Cooper had been back on the Diamond D, he'd noticed plenty of things Emily needed. But not until this moment did he realize just how much she'd done without and sacrificed so that the old ranch might survive. The whole idea filled him with shame and anger and an unexpected need to protect and care for her.

"Well, I guess they'll have to do for the time being," he said more gruffly than he'd intended, then helped her into the cab of the truck.

"So how did your visit with the doctor go?" he asked as they left the clinic parking lot.

"Dear heaven, I've gained eight pounds! When I stepped on those scales, I couldn't believe it."

Cooper could believe it. He'd noticed how her appetite had picked up and her body had blossomed from the nourishment. Her face had lost its gaunt look and her arms and shoulders were no longer bony. Then there was her tummy, which had grown much more obvious beneath her clothing. Most of her sweaters and shirts barely stretched across her now.

"You're supposed to gain weight," he reasoned. "You don't want to have a scrawny, sickly baby."

She placed her hand over her abdomen. "You sound like Dr. Bellamy. And you're right. I don't care if I look like a blimp afterward. I just want him to be healthy."

He looked at her with raised brows. It was the first time she'd ever mentioned the baby's sex. In fact, she rarely mentioned her pregnancy at all around him. He didn't know why and he wasn't at all sure he wanted to know.

"Did the doctor tell you it's going to be a boy?"

Emily shook her head. "No. I told him not to tell me. I want it to be a surprise. But deep down, I think it's a boy."

Cooper kept his eyes fixed on the traffic as he headed the truck onto one of Ruidoso's main streets. "Is a boy what you want?"

Surprised that he was even interested enough to ask, she looked at him. "The sex doesn't matter...I'll be happy with either."

*Happy.* Kenneth's child would make her happy. Why did the idea cut into him so? He'd never thought of himself as a mean or selfish man, but after living with Emily these past weeks he was having to take a second look at himself. God help him, he wanted her to be happy. She'd already had her share of heartaches. But why did she have to be pregnant with Kenneth's child? It wasn't that he'd hated his brother. But for as long as Cooper could remember, Kenneth had taken everything he'd ever wanted. His father's affection, The Diamond D and most of all, Emily.

Whether his brother had purposely coveted anything Cooper had ever touched, or whether Fate had simply stepped in and given it all to Kenneth, he didn't know. But either way Cooper felt cheated and wronged. The baby Emily was carrying should have rightfully been his. Instead Kenneth was still haunting him, still getting and taking even though he was gone from this earth.

Trying to shake his dark thoughts, he asked Emily, "Is there anything else you need to do in town?"

"Not really. I suppose I should go by the grocery store. I still have some things I want to do, anyway."

Nodding, she kept her surprise to herself. Try as she might she could never figure out what Cooper was feeling or thinking. And ever since that day the two of them had kissed in the tack room, he'd been even harder to figure. True, he'd kept his distance from her. The few times he had touched her was only in a distant manner, as one might touch a very old or very young person who needed a helping hand. But his words and tone had become far less biting now and he seemed to actually care if she was warm or cold or hungry or hurting. Moreover, he appeared to be content with his life on the Diamond D and that in itself surprised her more than anything.

A few moments later he braked the truck to a halt in front of one of the larger grocery stores in town.

"Twenty minutes will be plenty of time," she told him as she opened the door and slid to the ground.

"I may not be finished by then. Why don't you go to

the beauty salon next door and get your hair done while you wait on me.''

Her face screwed up with comical disbelief. ''Cooper, have you gone crazy or something?'' she asked, then tentatively touched her hand to her French braid. It was clean and neat. Or at least she thought it had been. ''Or do I look that bad?''

Snow was falling on her wool cap and shoulders and her breaths made little puffs of steam in the cold air. Looking at her, Cooper wanted to shake her and kiss her and tell her she was the most beautiful woman he'd ever known. Instead he raised up off the seat and dug his wallet out of the back pocket of his jeans. ''Here,'' he said, throwing a couple of large bills at her. ''Do as I say and don't argue.''

Her mouth fell open as she picked up the money. ''But Cooper—''

''Damn it, get inside before you freeze to death!''

Glowering at him, she slammed the door shut, then mouthed through the window at him. ''Gladly!''

After he'd driven away and Emily had collected her senses, she decided to go to the salon first and pick up the groceries she needed last.

A young hairdresser reading a tabloid magazine perked up when she spotted Emily coming through the salon doors. Tossing the sheets of gossip aside, the woman rose from the dryer chair. ''Can I help you?'' she asked pleasantly.

''I'm not sure. Do you have time to do my hair?'' Emily asked as she glanced around the large room decorated in shades of pink and white. It was a rare day when Emily went to a hair salon and she'd never been in this particular place. She had no idea if she could trust her hair to any of the three women. But she was here and it had been a long time since she'd had a good trim. Now was her best chance to get one.

''Sure. Why don't you get unwrapped and come sit down by the shampoo bowls,'' she cheerfully invited.

Still uncertain, Emily slowly took off her wool cap and coat and hung it on a nearby rack. When she turned back around, the hairdresser was patting the chair in a way that made her think of her first visit to the dentist.

"I really don't know what I'm doing in here," Emily said as she took a seat and the woman began to fasten a plastic cape around her neck. "I don't do anything to my hair except wash and brush it. Maybe you could just trim the dead ends. That should do it."

"Oh, surely you'd like to do something a little bit different." The woman's nimble fingers began to unbraid Emily's long hair. "Do you always wear it pulled back?"

Emily nodded and wondered why she felt like she'd been committing a crime. "I...don't have much time to spend on my hair."

"Hmm. None of us do. And even if we do, we don't like to." She lowered Emily's head back into one of the pink shampoo bowls.

"I'm going to have a baby the first part of March," Emily felt inclined to warn her. "So I don't want anything that requires a lot of care."

"Oh, a new baby! Well, this calls for something extra special," she exclaimed. "And I know just what you need."

The "something" pushed a panic button in Emily. Her eyes darted to the girl's name tag pinned to the pocket of her white uniform. "Uh, Lori, I don't think I need anything special."

"Nonsense!" She blasted Emily's scalp with a spray of warm water. "You're too pretty to be pulling your hair back in a braid every day. And I promise, once I get through with you, I'll bet your husband will agree. He won't be able to keep his hands off you."

Emily opened her mouth to tell her she didn't have a husband, then just as quickly closed it. She didn't want to explain anything about being a widow. For the next few minutes she simply wanted to enjoy being a woman and try not to think about Cooper's hands on her now or in the past.

A little more than an hour later, Emily climbed back into the pickup and fastened her seat belt.

Cooper stared at her as if he wasn't quite sure he'd picked up the right woman. "You are Emily Dunn, aren't you?" he asked. "And where's your cap?"

She shook the snowflakes from her hair. "That's the problem about a woman getting a hairdo. It makes her lose all common sense. My cap is in my coat when it should be on my head. But I didn't want to hurt the hairdresser's feelings by ruining all her hard work."

His gray eyes continued to roam over her hair, which had been shortened to frame her face and rest on the tops of her shoulders.

His scrutiny brought a warm blush to Emily's face, making her feel like a foolish schoolgirl. "Don't look at me like that."

"Like what?"

Why didn't he put the pickup in gear and go? The grocery attendant had already loaded her few sacks in the back of the vehicle. There was no reason for them to keep hanging around in the parking lot.

"Like I've suddenly grown a set of horns or something," she told him crossly.

He laughed, then shook his head. "Emily, I can't figure out whether you've grown incredibly young or ridiculously old. But either way, you look very pretty."

She hadn't thought of getting a compliment from him. Nor had she expected it to fill her with such pleasure. What was the matter with her anyway?

Jerking her eyes off him, she stared out the windshield. She'd never been a woman to primp and fuss. From the age of seven to thirteen she'd grown up without a mother. During that time her father had taught her to be a cowgirl, nothing more. Later, Rose had come into their lives, but by that time Emily supposed she was too much of a tomboy to ever become a feminine fashion plate.

"Thank you, Cooper. Now can we go home?"

Home. Cooper had never believed that word would sound good to him. Especially when it was connected to the Diamond D. But more and more when he heard Emily say it, he got a warm feeling in the middle of his chest.

He was beginning to feel as if the old ranch was his home again, that being there with Emily was right and natural. Yet he knew those feelings had to stop or he was going to be in deep trouble.

Ever since he'd kissed Emily more than a month ago, he'd decided his time on the Diamond D had to be limited. As soon as the baby got here and she could do for herself, he had to leave. Maybe that was the cowardly way out for him, but the way he saw things, there was no other course for him to take. It was already becoming an effort to keep his hands off her. Nor could he bear to stay and watch her with Kenneth's baby. Either way he was damned and there wasn't a thing he could do to change it.

"Yeah, I think it's time we got home," he said.

That evening while Emily was cooking supper, Cooper carried a large box and several sacks into the kitchen and placed them on the table.

"What's all that? Early Christmas shopping?"

He gave her a sly little smile. "I guess you could call it that." With his head he motioned for her to come there. Emily laid down her turning fork and walked over to where he stood by the table.

"What is it?" she asked. "I can't let the steaks burn. All the other meat I bought is frozen."

"I'll tend to the steaks, you see if you can use any of these things."

More than curious, she dug into the first sack and immediately let out a loud gasp. It was maternity clothes! Quickly she looked in the next sack and the next. There were all sorts of slacks made of warm corduroy, velvet and knit, sweaters of cotton and cashmere, and dresses of soft jersey.

Looking up at him with shocked eyes, she asked, "Where did all this come from?"

"Don't worry about that. Will the things fit?"

This afternoon in Ruidoso he'd said he had something else to do while she finished her shopping. She couldn't believe he'd gone to a boutique and bought her these things! Her mind spinning with questions, she glanced at the tags inside the garments. They were all pretty much her size.

"Yes, they'll fit. But—"

"Open the box."

"The steaks—"

Waving away her protest, he went over to the stove to tend the frying meat. "Okay, they're not burning. Now open the box."

Like a kid at Christmas, Emily didn't have to be told a second time. She tore into the box, then simply stared at the contents.

"What's the matter? Wrong color?"

Slowly she lifted the red wool coat from its nest of tissue paper, then held it in front of her. It was a classic cut that buttoned down the front and stopped just above her ankles. The fabric was tightly woven, not only making it baby soft, but also very warm.

Tears stung her throat as she looked at him. Her mother had given her things she needed from time to time, but this wasn't the same. Not nearly the same. "The coat is beautiful, Cooper. But I don't understand—"

"There's something else in the box," he interrupted.

Carefully lying the garment to one side, Emily peeled back another layer of tissue paper. "Snow boots!"

Quickly she kicked off her loafers and pushed her feet into the black, fur lined boots. The warmth of them was like heaven against her toes. "Oooh," she exclaimed, "these feel delicious."

"Then they fit?"

"I think so. Let me see." She zipped the sides, then tentatively walked across the kitchen floor. "They're perfect. How did you know what size to get? And my clothes?"

He gave her a lopsided smile. "I have a good eye."

Laughing with disbelief, she pulled on the coat, buttoned it, then turned slowly in front of him. "How do I look? Like a fat red robin?"

She looked like the Emily he used to know, the happy laughing woman that had stolen his breath away. "You look...beautiful."

She laughed again as though she didn't believe him about that either and hurried toward the door. When she started to step outside he asked, "Where are you going?"

"I'm going out to see how my coat and boots work."

"They'll work fine," he said, shaking his head with comical disbelief. "It's too cold to be going out now!"

Ignoring his objection, she shut the door behind her.

Cursing, Cooper forked the steaks onto a platter and hurried after her. When he stepped onto the small square porch, he saw Emily out in the yard dancing happily around in the snow.

"I can't feel a thing," she called. "I'm as warm as toast and my feet are as dry as powder!"

"That's good. Now get—"

Suddenly her footing slipped, but she managed to right herself before falling. Instantly Cooper leapt off the porch and grabbed her around her thick waist before she knew what was happening.

"Damn it, girl, what are you trying to do? Hurt yourself and the baby?"

The harsh tone of his voice broke the happy spell his gifts had given her. As she looked up at his dark face, she wondered how she could have forgotten, even for a moment, the pain this man had caused her. "You would say something like that now," she said through tight lips. "Now that it's too late."

His face wrinkled with confusion. "What?"

She tried to push his arms away from her. "Let me go! I can get back in the house myself!"

Ignoring her efforts to get away, he guided her up the steps and into the warm kitchen. However, once they were inside with the door shut, he still refused to let her go.

"I asked you a question, Emily. What were you talking about out there? What did you mean, too late? Are you keeping something from me about your visit with Dr. Bellamy today?"

"No! And what would you care anyway? You wouldn't give a damn if I lost this baby, too!"

As soon as she realized what she'd said, her mouth fell open and every last drop of color drained from her face. For a moment Cooper thought she was going to faint and he tightened his hold on the sides of her waist.

"This baby, too? Were you pregnant before?"

There was no point in trying to hide it now, Emily thought. She'd already let too much slip. She knew Cooper wouldn't quit until she answered him.

Nodding stiffly, she whispered, "Yes."

"When?" he demanded.

"A long time ago."

Her evasive answer caused him to give her shoulders a little shake. "How long ago? Tell me, Emily?"

She sagged against the crook of his arm. "What does it matter, Cooper? You didn't care. You had already gone."

Stunned, he lifted his eyes to the ceiling. "It was...my baby?"

"Yes."

His eyes jerked back down to hers. "And you didn't tell me! Why?" he asked hoarsely.

Her face felt frozen while inside her heart was so full of pain she thought it was going to splinter right down the middle. "Because when I found out I was pregnant you had already left Lincoln county. So I didn't tell anyone, not even my parents or aunts. I didn't want anyone knowing I'd made the gullible mistake of sleeping with a man who didn't love me."

"You're wrong—"

"I don't want to hear it!" Pushing out of his grasp, she hurriedly left the room.

Minutes ticked by as Cooper tried to digest all that she'd just told him, but it was so hard for him to imagine Emily suffering the pain and heartache of losing a baby. His baby! Oh, God, if only he'd known! No wonder she hated him.

Their supper forgotten, Cooper left the kitchen and walked down a long hallway to where the bedrooms were located. He found Emily in hers, lying across the bed. She was still wearing the coat and boots he'd bought for her.

Her face was turned down to the mattress and the slight tremor of her shoulders told him she was crying. He felt like a jerk for ever hurting her, yet he couldn't help but be angry with her, too. She'd shut him out, chosen not to tell him about their baby. The mere idea crushed him.

"Emily."

She turned her head slightly and looked at him. "Get out!"

"No. Like you told me before, you can't open a can of worms then just walk away." He went over and sat down on the side of the bed. "You shouldn't be crying. It isn't good for you."

She flopped onto her back and her wet eyes clashed with his. "I shouldn't even be pregnant! That's what Kenneth told me when he found out about the coming baby."

Shaking his head, he said gently, "Emily, don't do this—"

"I have to do it," she interrupted. "You wanted to know, so you need to know all of it."

Cooper started to tell her he didn't need to know anything just so she would calm herself. But then it dawned on him that she probably needed to tell him, she needed to share the burden of her pain with him.

"Okay. Tell me," he murmured.

She scrubbed her eyes with her fists, but fresh tears reappeared as soon as she looked at him. Cooper felt sick and helpless.

"For a long time after you left, Kenneth didn't know you and I had been lovers. He hadn't realized we'd gotten that close and I didn't tell him until—one day he came by the ranch. I hadn't seen him in a while and I suppose the sight of him only reminded me of you even more. I don't know. But anyway I was in a particularly low mood and started crying in front of him. When he began to question me, I broke down and told him about the baby."

"I see. You could tell him. But you couldn't tell me," he said accusingly.

Her eyes lifted to his face. It was full of bitterness and she had to wonder what her confession was doing to him. It was hard for her to believe he might have cared back then.

"You weren't around. Remember?"

"I could have been found!"

She groaned. "If a man has to be tracked down to be told he's going to be a father, then it's pretty obvious he wasn't interested in the first place!"

"I wrote you. You knew I hadn't gone off with intentions of forgetting you," he argued.

Emily sighed. "The only thing you ever talked about in those few letters I got was about the next rodeo you were going to or the one you'd just left. And about the money you were winning. Nothing about us or when you would be coming back.''

"What the hell did you want me to talk about? It would have been wrong of me to make promises to you when I didn't know where or when my next dollar was coming from." He grimaced as his eyes scanned her pale face. "But I guess Kenneth knew exactly what to say to you. He must have made damn quick work of proposing to you.''

"He was concerned about me and the baby. He said he wanted to take care of us.''

Cooper's eyes narrowed to calculating slits. "Why? Did he think I couldn't?''

She opened her mouth to respond, but he quickly shook his head, then turned his head away from her. "There's no need to answer that," he said in a low, gritty voice. "I think I'm finally beginning to see how things really were.''

"What do you mean, really were?''

He looked back at her and Emily could see his gray eyes were roiling with emotions she couldn't begin to understand.

"Kenneth was just like our old man,'' he said flatly. "He didn't think I could handle the responsibility.''

Emily's brow puckered. "I don't think that was the case at all. He simply thought you were no longer interested in me. And he knew I didn't want to force you into coming back and marrying me simply for the sake of the baby. I didn't want you that way.''

Incensed, his nostrils flared. No one, especially Emily, had understood what had really been in Cooper's heart back then. Kenneth should have contacted him and let him know about Emily's condition. But he hadn't. Instead he'd married Emily himself. Maybe his motive had been concern, as Emily seemed to think, but Cooper was beginning to see it as something else entirely.

"So you married Kenneth and let everyone think it was his baby you were carrying?''

Her head swung sadly back and forth. "No. It didn't happen that way, Coop. I couldn't bear to think of marrying another man. Not while I was carrying your child. I kept holding out—hoping you'd come back. I was only a couple of months into the pregnancy and no one but Kenneth knew about it. But then I had a spontaneous miscarriage and was forced into going to see Dr. Bellamy to make sure I was all right. With Aunt Justine being his nurse, I could hardly hide what had happened from her. But she's respected my privacy all these years. No one else in my family knows about it."

Cooper was quiet for long moments as he tried to take in all that she'd just told him. "You didn't marry Kenneth because you were pregnant. So why did you marry him?"

In the past few years, Emily had asked herself that question a thousand times over. She still wasn't exactly certain why, except that Kenneth had caught her at a very vulnerable time in her life. She'd lost Cooper and then their baby. She'd needed someone and something to believe in and Kenneth had sworn to always love her.

"He seemed to care about me and he thought we could have a good marriage. You were out of my life and he wanted me in spite of losing the baby."

He made a snorting sound. "How noble of him."

"It was more than I got out of you," she returned.

Maybe it had been, Cooper thought. But only because his brother had chosen to exclude him, once again. It made him wonder what else had gone on with Kenneth that he hadn't known about.

Emily's sigh brought him out of his thoughts and he looked at her with such deep regret that tears welled up in her eyes.

"If it's any consolation our marriage was never rosy. He didn't say it often, but for all these years Kenneth believed I was still carrying you around in my heart."

Had she really been carrying him around in her heart all

this time? Cooper wondered. It was hard to imagine. More often than not she seemed to despise him.

Emily went on, "And then it didn't help matters when I couldn't conceive. Kenneth had the idea that the miscarriage I suffered with your baby had damaged me somehow. But I—"

He looked at her sharply. "It wasn't the reason you couldn't conceive, was it? I mean, you're pregnant now."

Emily sighed and Cooper was grateful to see her tears were drying and she was far more composed than when he first entered the bedroom.

"Dr. Bellamy assures me the miscarriage had nothing to do with it. He simply believes Kenneth wasn't very fertile. We'll never know because he refused to be tested. But as far as I'm concerned that's all just medical jargon anyway. *I* was the reason I couldn't give Kenneth a child. I had sinned with you and that was my retribution."

Cooper had never imagined that Emily might be blaming herself. Him, most surely. But not herself. "That's crazy talk!"

"Is it?" she countered. "You don't feel any regret or guilt for making love to me all those years ago?"

Groaning, he reached over and pushed his fingers through the side of her hair. "Emily, there's nothing sinful about two people loving each other. The only thing I regret is…that you didn't wait on me. And if I'd known about the baby—"

"I told you before, I didn't want you that way," she whispered fiercely. "If you didn't care enough about me to stay, I certainly wasn't going to drag you back by forcing the responsibility of a child on you."

His fingers left her hair and traced a gentle pattern over her cheek. "I was coming back. I know you don't believe me—"

"But when? Whenever you grew tired of being a rodeo

star?'' She shook her head. ''I needed more than a vague promise from you, Cooper.''

''Do you think I left this place just to chase after some cockeyed dream? I left so I could eventually give you more.''

Grabbing his hand, she gripped it as her eyes searched his. ''You still don't understand, Cooper. I didn't need material things from you. I needed a commitment from you.''

He had been committed to her. But obviously she hadn't been able to see what was in his heart way back then. She'd taken his leaving as a sign of desertion. And now it was too late to change the past.

His eyes fixed on a spot of the bedspread, he absently rubbed his fingers over the back of her hand. ''And I needed to be able to offer you more than just me, Emily. Cooper Dunn by himself wasn't good enough for a woman like you.''

The picture he was trying to paint for her was suddenly unfolding in her mind and she shut her eyes, hoping it would block out the painful image. ''Oh, Coop,'' she whispered brokenly. ''How did things between us get so messed up?''

Cooper was tired of trying to understand why or how any of it had ever happened. Right now all he wanted was to hold her, feel the reassuring warmth of her body against him.

She didn't resist when he pulled her into his arms. For long moments he simply held her head against his shoulder and buried his face in the silky fall of her hair. But after a while he realized she'd started to cry again.

Easing her head back, he wiped the teardrops from her cheeks, then bending his head, he placed a kiss on her pale forehead.

''Don't cry, my darling. Please don't cry.''

''Oh, Coop,'' she suddenly wailed, then flung her arms around his neck. ''Love me!''

Cooper didn't bother to question her invitation. He needed her too much. Easing her back down on the mattress, he framed her face with both hands.

"I'm not supposed to love you, Emily," he murmured against her lips. "But I can't seem to help myself."

Gripping his neck, Emily urged him closer, opened her mouth to the hard line of his. She'd never needed him so much or wanted him this badly.

Her eagerness didn't surprise Cooper. Somewhere deep inside him, he'd known, just as she knew that the fire between them had never died. But the urgency of her soft lips against his mouth, his face and neck was filling him with heat, making it impossible to pull away from her.

Like a starved man, he drank over and over from her lips while his hands crushed her hair in both fists. Eventually her fingers were loosening the buttons of his flannel shirt, tugging the tails from his jeans, then sliding across his hard abdomen.

"Emily," he groaned against her throat. "You know I can't resist you."

"I don't want you to," she murmured. Her hands slid up his chest, then rested against his flat nipples.

Groaning in his throat, Cooper tried to remember any other time he'd felt as he did now. He was consumed with physical desire and yet there was so much more inside him. His heart ached with the need to give her comfort and pleasure and joy. He'd never felt like this with any woman. And he knew if he lived until the end of time, he never would.

With his lips still fastened hungrily to hers, he loosened the buttons on her coat. Sensing his need, Emily raised up enough to allow him to slip the coat off her shoulders. As soon as he'd tossed the garment out of the way, he lay down beside her and pulled her into the tight circle of his arms.

Emily pressed herself against him and reveled in the hard

length of his body. It had been so long since she'd felt like this—like a woman.

As his lips continued to feast on hers, his hands stroked her back, then slid beneath her sweater and around to her breast. After encountering the thin barrier of lace, his fingers fumbled urgently with the clasp of her bra until the material finally fell away and his hands could touch her freely.

Her breasts were full and heavy in his palms, her nipples rigid against the pads of his thumbs. Moaning low in her throat, Emily eased far enough away from him to slip the sweater over her head. The sight of her in the dim lamplight made his breath catch in his throat.

"You're more lovely than I ever remembered," he murmured, then dipping his head he kissed one smooth breast.

Emily dug her fingers into his dark hair. "Do you know how often I've dreamed of being with you again...like this?"

"Not nearly as much as I have," he said hoarsely, then pressing her flat against the mattress, he found her mouth again.

Then as he eased himself over the length of her, he felt it. The soft mound of her belly pushing against him. The baby. Kenneth's baby. How could he have forgotten? How could he be making love to her while she carried another man's baby?

The desire that had been pulsing through his veins like hot lava instantly turned to ice water. With a moan of self-disgust he rolled away from her. His breaths coming hard and fast, he stared up at the ceiling.

"I'm sorry, Emily, I—"

Befuddled by the sudden separation of their bodies, she raised up on her elbow and looked at him. "Cooper? What's wrong?"

Cooper cut his gaze back to her face and immediately felt a lance of regret at the passion he saw etched on her

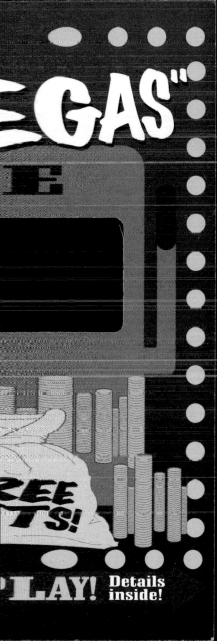

features. She wanted him! Just knowing that ought to be enough for him. But it wasn't. He couldn't take what she so readily offered, then later walk away. He'd already hurt her far more than he could bear to think about. Yet he couldn't stay. He wasn't emotionally fit to be her husband or the father of her baby. Not while every part of his heart was filled with resentment. For years he'd played the whipping boy, the second son beneath Kenneth. He didn't want to be the second husband or a stand-in father. He'd be miserable if he tried.

"I just can't do this," he said lowly.

Leaning closer, she placed her hand upon his chest. She could feel the rapid thud of his heart and beneath the evening shadow of his beard, his face had paled.

"Are you ill?" she asked worriedly.

Unable to hold her gaze, he glanced at her small hand resting in the middle of his chest. "No. I'm—"

"You realize you don't want to make love to me. Is that it?" Her voice was low and hoarse as though it hurt to speak.

Cooper shook his head. "I do want to make love to you, Emily. More than anything. But I'm not going to. Now or ever."

She didn't say anything and eventually Cooper turned on his side to face her. His gray eyes shadowed with pain, he reached over and gently touched her swollen belly.

"Cooper," she began before he could, "It's perfectly natural for pregnant women to make love."

"It isn't that. It's...the baby reminded me of Kenneth. Of all the—"

Her eyes grew wide as the meaning of his words sunk in on her. "If that's the way you feel then why...why did you pretend to want me when—"

"Damn it all, I do want you! But..."

Grabbing her sweater, she jerked it over her head. "I'm sorry you're repulsed by the sight of my body. I'm sorry you can't deal with the fact that I'm carrying Kenneth's baby. But it's *my* baby, too. And when it gets here it will still be my baby. If you can't deal with that, maybe you should leave. That seems to solve your problems, anyway."

Rising to his feet, his eyes searched her face. "I've already planned to leave once the baby is born. I just hadn't told you yet."

So that was the way it was with him, Emily thought, as she gazed up at his dark face. Time hadn't changed him at all. His plans were no different than they'd been ten years ago. He was going to leave.

"Well, I shouldn't be surprised," she said, her voice going flat as all the emotion seemed to drain out of her. "But I am. I thought...foolish me, I believed you were starting to fit in here. That you even liked living here on the ranch again...with me."

"I do like it! I just can't stay here after the baby comes."

His words brought her to her feet. "What are you saying? That you're going to let one little innocent baby come between us? A baby that, I might add, needs a father?"

Oh God, why had all this happened, he silently prayed. And why couldn't he be the man she needed?

"I told you before, Emily. I'm not father material."

"Because it's Kenneth's baby?"

He turned away from her but not before she saw his features twisting with frustration. "I might as well tell you like it is. I'm not sure I could be a good father to any child. Besides that, I don't think I could bring myself to love and nurture—Kenneth's child. Not after the way he betrayed me!"

She wished she had the strength to slap him. But the past few minutes had drained her physically and emotionally. All she could manage to do was look at him with dark, wounded eyes. "If that's the way you feel, why don't you go on and leave now? I wish you would! I wish I never had to see your selfish face again!"

She whirled her back to him.

Cooper stood where he was while his eyes took in the angry rigid line of her stance. He wished there was something he could say or do to comfort her, to make up for all the things she'd wanted from him. But he didn't know how or what. He supposed he wasn't any better in dealing with women than he was with children. He was a man meant to be alone.

Stepping closer, he placed his hand on her shoulder. "Right now you need me here as much as I need to be here," he murmured.

She twisted her head around and glared at him. "And you believe I won't need you after the baby gets here? With thinking like that I'll be better off once you're gone!"

His stiff features hid the pain in his heart. "I'm sure you'll be counting the days."

# Chapter Six

Emily was on that damn Appaloosa again. Cooper knew she was an excellent rider and had been since she was a small child. He also had to admit the weather wasn't all that bad for the end of November. But she was pregnant, for heaven's sake! She should be in the house knitting or whatever it was women did when they were in the family way. But no, not her, he thought as he watched her from an inconspicuous place in the barn. Emily was a ranch woman inside and out. If she wasn't helping him feed and care for the cattle, she was doing something with the horses or the tack.

Cooper had quit trying to send her back to the house. Especially after the encounter they'd had in her bedroom over two weeks ago. Since then, Cooper had come to the conclusion that he didn't have the right to tell her anything. He wasn't her husband. Nor the father of her child. He wasn't even her lover. He was, in spite of ten years passing, just what he'd always been here on the Diamond D. An interloper. Yet he couldn't leave. His conscience wouldn't let him. Or was it his heart?

Deciding it was time he made an appearance, he walked out to the big round pen where she was exercising the horse. Resting his forearms over the metal rail fencing, he watched her rein the gelding first one way and then the other.

It was only a moment before she noticed his presence and walked the horse over to him.

"He handles very well," Cooper told her.

She smiled. "Thank you. I believe he's going to be my kind of pony. I almost wish it was roundup time so I could really give him a good workout. If he's going to show his true colors it will be then."

By roundup time in the spring, Emily's baby would be born. She'd be able to ride as long and far as she wanted. And Cooper would be gone. He didn't want to think about it, but he had to.

"Maybe the calf crop will be a good one come this spring."

Emily looked down at him from atop the horse. Oddly enough she felt closer to him now than she ever had. Which didn't make sense. That night in her bedroom his rejection had cut her to the quick. But afterward, when she'd had time to cool off and really think, her anger at him had vanished.

Emily had concluded it was probably for the best the two of them hadn't made love. Cooper couldn't let go of the past. And she wasn't at all sure she could forget it, either. He'd left her when she'd needed him the most. And more than likely he would do it again.

"If we don't have any late blizzards I think the calf crop will be a good one. As good as it can be with only a hundred mama cows." Carefully she stepped down from the saddle and looped the reins over the metal fence.

"I've been thinking about adding to the herd," Cooper told her. "I doubt cattle will be any lower than they are right now. It would be a good time to buy. But..."

He didn't go on and she looked at him questioningly. "But what?"

"I don't want to take the step until I know for sure I can find a good man to work the place for you."

Whenever he left, Emily silently added. The thought saddened her, though she didn't know why she should let it. He kept her emotions in constant turmoil. And the desire she felt for him was something she couldn't stop no matter how hard she tried.

"You haven't forgotten tomorrow is Thanksgiving, have you?"

"No. Would you like to go out somewhere to eat?"

"Thank you for asking, but that wasn't really what I had in mind. You see, my family always gathers at the Bar M for the holidays and we're invited."

His brows lifted slightly. "'*We?*' You really mean you, don't you?"

Emily shook her head. "No. You've been invited, too. Why should that surprise you?"

"I figured your whole family thought of me as that Dunn bastard."

"Cooper!" she scolded.

"Especially your father."

Emily shook her head. "Daddy's been over here several times in the past few weeks and you two seem to get along, okay."

"Your father is a nice man. He just doesn't say what's really on his mind."

Emily laughed. "Daddy is a nice man. But don't let that niceness fool you. If he gets riled up, he doesn't hide it."

Cooper let out a sigh and pushed his hat to the back of his head. Strands of dark hair flopped onto his forehead. "That may be true. But I just don't think I'd feel comfortable having Thanksgiving dinner with your family."

She folded her arms across her breast. "Just who would you feel comfortable with, Cooper?"

Shrugging, he jammed his hands into the pockets of his jeans and stared off at the distant Capitan mountains. "I don't know. I guess some of the old cowboys I travel with."

Several of those old cowboys had called Cooper in the past couple of months he'd been here on the Diamond D. A few times Emily had heard him laughing and joking with the person on the other end of the line and she'd felt absurdly jealous. Even now it was on the tip of her tongue to tell him he was welcome to go spend Thanksgiving with his rodeo buddies, but she caught herself before the words were out.

As she stood there looking at his remote expression, she realized Cooper was being totally honest with her. For the past ten years he'd not had a family to speak of, or a home to go to for the holidays. At least, a home where he'd felt as if he were truly welcome. Had she been the reason? Had he not wanted to see her and Kenneth together? Dear Lord she might be crazy, but she was beginning to think he might have actually loved her after all.

"Well, I'm sure your rodeo buddies have been missing you. But since you're here, it would make me very happy if you'd spend the day with my family."

*Happy.* She'd never mentioned him and the word in the same breath. That she was doing so now, more than surprised him.

"I don't know, Emily. I wouldn't want to…make your relatives uncomfortable."

"Why would you make them uncomfortable? Except for Aunt Justine and my parents, they all think you're just one of my old boyfriends."

*Just an old boyfriend.* Sometimes Cooper wondered if he'd ever been that much to her. "I understand that Justine knows we were lovers, but what did your parents think I was? Other than sorry and no good."

"They thought…" She drew in a breath and glanced

away from him. "They thought you were the man I ought to have married. Not Kenneth. They both desperately tried to talk me out of marrying him. But I was so hurt over you, I wouldn't listen." She turned her eyes back on him. "So you see, they didn't think you were sorry or not good enough. They believed you were the man for me. And I think they...still believe you are."

Cooper didn't know what to say. It touched him to think the Hamiltons had once wanted him for a son-in-law. But now...how could he accompany Emily to a family gathering as though he belonged there, too? He'd not only let Emily down years ago, he'd obviously disappointed Harlan and Rose, two people he greatly admired. If only they knew he'd left all those years ago out of love, he thought dismally.

Tugging his hat back on his head, he said, "If that's the case, they'd probably be happier if you show up alone. But," he added as her face fell with disappointment, "I'll think about it."

"You can't think on it long. Tomorrow is Thanksgiving and if I stay here and cook for the two of us, I'll have to drive into town for a turkey."

Surprise flickered over his face. "I wouldn't expect you to stay here and cook for me."

"Well, I would hardly go off and leave you."

She seemed adamant about the whole thing, though Cooper couldn't understand why. They'd never spent a holiday together, so he could hardly imagine her wanting them to now.

"All right. If that's the way you feel, I'll let you know in a little while." He reached for the Appaloosa's reins. "Are you finished riding? I'll put him up for you."

Emily knew if Cooper had it his way she'd be in the house all day with her feet propped up. He'd not tried to hide the fact he resented her pregnancy. So why did he make such an issue of taking care of her health?

"Yes. I'm all through," she told him. "I'm going on up to the house to do a few chores."

She'd taken only a few steps in the direction of the house when Cooper called her name. Pausing, she twisted her head around at him. "Yes?"

"I just wanted to thank you for...wanting to share Thanksgiving with me."

A hot lump collected in her throat. Until this moment she'd never realized just how alone Cooper really was and how much she wanted to take away that loneliness by sharing her family with him. "You're welcome, Cooper."

Later that evening Emily was on the phone with her aunt Chloe when Cooper entered the kitchen.

"I don't know, Aunt Chloe—" She broke off the moment she heard the door closing behind him. "Huh—here he is now. Wait a minute." Emily placed her hand over the mouthpiece of the telephone. "What's your answer about dinner tomorrow?" she asked him. "Aunt Chloe needs to know how many chairs to drag out."

Even though he knew it was a special thing for Emily to spend the holidays with her family, she'd already made it clear to him she wouldn't leave him here alone. She would give up being with her family for him. That in itself touched him deeply. And what the hell if he didn't belong to the family? he argued with himself. Emily seemed to want him there and that was enough for him.

"Tell her to drag out two more. As long as I don't have to wear a tie," he added impishly.

Excitement suddenly gleamed in her eyes and for a moment Cooper thought she was going to jump up on her tiptoes and kiss him. But then she seemed to think better of it and turned her attention back to her aunt.

"We'll be there, Aunt Chloe. Cooper might be in his chaps and spurs, but I'll make sure he doesn't have any manure on his boots."

She hung up the phone and smiled at him. "I know you're dreading this, but it won't be nearly as bad as you think. If you get tired of the racket you can always go down to the stables and look at Chloe's horses. She has one barn full of nothing but yearlings."

Just seeing the smile on her face made it all worth it to Cooper. With a wry grin, he said, "Don't worry about me, Emily. Contrary to what you might think I can survive a few hours without a horse."

The Murdock family ranch was south and west of Hondo where the mountains were covered with ponderosa and piñon pine. Cooper had visited the Bar M once before when he'd first met Emily years ago. The vast ranch had been beautiful then, but it was even more so now, Cooper thought as he drove up the long pine-lined driveway leading to the house. He could see many improvements around the barns and stables. And when the two of them entered the courtyard at the back of the old Spanish-styled home, he noticed a huge oval swimming pool had been added.

The one time Cooper had visited the Bar M, the weather had been warm and the family had had a barbecue. Though he and Emily had only stayed for a few minutes, the experience had stuck in his memory. He'd never seen so much laughter and genuine closeness in a family before. To this day, he often tried to imagine what it must be like to be a part of such a supportive, tightly knit group of relatives.

"Did Kenneth get on with your family?" he asked as the two of them walked through the courtyard toward a door that would lead them into the kitchen.

She shrugged. "Kenneth never was much of a socializer. Most of the time I visited the family, he chose to stay home."

Her answer told Cooper that once again his assumptions about Kenneth had been wrong. "That surprises me. I figured Kenneth got on well with your folks."

"He did for a while. But the last few years he cut himself off from most everyone. Maybe the alcohol made him that way. I don't know." Shaking her head, she smiled up at him. "Let's not talk about such dismal things now. The day is beautiful and my mother and aunts have cooked a feast."

And for once Cooper wasn't spending Thanksgiving in a motel room eating fast food with a bunch of road-weary cowboys, he thought. He was with the woman he'd always wanted to be with and she was smiling at him. He couldn't ask for more than that.

Much to Emily's relief everyone in the family greeted Cooper warmly. Even though he'd met them all before, she'd wondered if he might have trouble remembering her brother, Ethan and all her cousins: Caroline, the twins, Adam and Anna, and their sister, Ivy. All of them had grown from teenagers to adulthood since he'd been away. But surprisingly he recognized them all and even inquired about Charlie, who hadn't been able to get away from his duties as a Texas Ranger.

"That's too bad," Cooper told Roy. "I would have enjoyed visiting with Charlie. I always liked him."

Roy glanced at Justine, who was trying to smile even though she was missing her son terribly, especially with it being a holiday. "We wish he could have been here, too. But he's been working on a case that's kept him pretty much tied down."

Across the room, Caroline chuckled slyly. "That's just what my brother is telling our parents," she told Cooper. "Frankly I think it's a woman that has him tied up."

"If that's the case," Justine spoke up, "then I forgive him for staying in Texas. I'm beginning to think that boy will never find a woman who'll put up with him."

Roy slid his arm around Justine's shoulders and gave his wife an affectionate squeeze. "It's because he's trying to find a perfect one like his mother."

Everyone groaned and laughed and swapped a few more remarks about Charlie, then the men eventually gravitated to the living room to have coffee. As Emily watched Cooper leave with them, a pang of regret coursed through her heart. He seemed to fit in with her family as though he'd always belonged to it. Whereas Kenneth had always been moody and distant whenever he'd been around the Murdock clan. The difference between the two men was as great as night and day and she was beginning to see more and more what a drastic mistake she'd made ten years ago when she'd fallen in with Kenneth's idea to get married.

Once the men were gone from the kitchen, Justine turned to Emily and slung a loving arm around her shoulders. "Emily, you look absolutely beautiful," Justine exclaimed. "I can't get over your hair. Isn't it lovely, Rose?"

"It is. But I'm still in shock over the coat. Where did you get it?" her mother asked.

Emily felt a blush rising to her cheeks. "Well, actually Cooper went shopping for me and this is one of the things he thought I needed." She unbuttoned the red coat and handed it to her Aunt Chloe who had yet to say anything, but was giving her a knowing little smile.

"Emily!" Rose whirled away from the gas range to give her daughter's dress a closer look. "That dress. It looks like cashmere!"

Laughing, Chloe patted Emily's rotund middle. "It feels like cashmere, too. I'll bet our little girl in there just loves it."

"How do you know it's going to be a girl?" Anna asked her mother as she, Ivy and Caroline pulled china and silverware from an antique buffet.

"I'm just guessing," Chloe answered her daughter's question. Justine stepped up and placed her hands on Emily's tummy as though she were calculating the ripeness of a watermelon. "You're wrong, sis. It's a boy. See how low she's carrying it."

Emily groaned, yet the smile on her face said how much she was enjoying the attention. "Oh, for goodness' sake, you'd think none of you had ever seen a pregnant woman before."

"Well, we haven't seen one in a while," Chloe exclaimed.

Laughing, Justine motioned to the three younger women. "We're still waiting for the tables to be set."

"But we wanted to ask Emily about Cooper," Anna complained as she waved a handful of forks at her mother. "He's gorgeous."

"And much too old for you," Chloe told her.

Anna turned to Emily. "Mother said he rode broncs in the PRCA, is that true? She said he was a champion!"

"That's true," Emily said, not a bit surprised at her young niece's interest in Cooper. He had that something about him that made women, young and old, look and wonder and sigh.

"Gosh, he must live an exciting life," Anna said with a sigh. "And to think he came back to be with you. I can't imagine a man doing that for me."

Chloe rolled her eyes at her daughter's exaggerated comment. "That's because you haven't met the right man yet. Now you girls go get the tables ready. The food is going to get cold if we have to keep waiting on you three."

The young women, who all happened to be different shades of redheads like their mothers, left the room. Once they were out of sight, Emily made a helpless gesture with her hands. "I should have told Anna that Cooper didn't come home for me. But I guess she'd have romantic notions in her head no matter what I said."

"She is that age," Chloe agreed with a resigned shake of her head. "And now that her piano concerts have her traveling from coast to coast, I can only hope she doesn't lose her head over the wrong one."

"The same goes for my Caroline," Justine added, then

glancing to make sure there was no one else in earshot except her sisters, she said to Emily, "Okay. The girls are gone now. So you can tell your mother and your aunts how things really are."

"Really are?" Laughing awkwardly, Emily walked over to the gas range where the baked turkey was keeping warm on a huge platter. She sniffed the delicious aroma. "Things are just what you see," she told her. "Cooper is trying to get the ranch back in shape and I'm helping him up to a point. He won't let me do much without an argument."

"How long is he going to stay?" Chloe asked. "He has a career men would pull their eyeteeth for. We're all surprised he's stayed away from it this long."

Rather than look at the three older women, Emily examined every dish of food on the cabinet counter. Along with the turkey there was baked ham, candied sweet potatoes, corn bread dressing and giblet gravy, plus an endless number of salads and vegetables.

Eventually she said, "Cooper is going to stay for a while yet. Until the baby comes."

"And what then?" Justine questioned.

Emily knew her aunts loved her very much and they were only asking her these questions out of concern for her. But Emily didn't want to talk about Cooper leaving. She didn't like to think how quiet the house would be without him. Or how it would be to get up every morning and not see his face or hear his voice. At night when she went to bed, he wouldn't be in the bedroom across the hall.

"He's going to hire a man to run the place and he's…going back to rodeoing, I guess."

"Hmm, that doesn't make much sense to me," Chloe said thoughtfully. "If he plans to go back to his career in rodeo, looks like he'd do it now before the finals in Las Vegas. He could hire someone to work on the ranch now as well as later. If he stays here with you, he stands to lose a lot of money."

"I've pointed all that out to him, Aunt Chloe. But he has his own ideas."

"And I think all those ideas are about you," Justine remarked.

Emily groaned. For the life of her she didn't know why her relatives had these romantic ideas about her and Cooper. "You don't know what you're talking about."

Justine rolled her eyes. "Oh, no? Just take another look at the dress you have on," she told Emily.

Emily glanced down at the teal green sweater dress, which was cut to gently drape her growing figure. "I can see it's very nice."

"Nice!" Justine burst out with disbelief. "I wish Roy had that much taste. The last thing he bought me was two sizes too small and was a garish orange color. He thought it would go with my hair. But I did my best to act like I loved it."

Emily sighed. "Believe me, Cooper bought clothes for me simply because he knew I needed them. That's all there is to it. There's no other underlying reason. So please, no more trying to link the two of us together. It just isn't going to happen. Now when are we going to eat?"

As if on cue Ivy stuck her head over the batwing doors leading into the kitchen. "The tables are ready and the men are getting restless."

"Okay honey," Chloe told her. "We're bringing the food out now."

Relieved the interrogation about Cooper was over, Emily picked up a bowl of fruit salad and hurried out of the room. She had almost reached the dining table when her mother caught up to her and took her to one side.

"Don't be upset with your aunts, darling," she said in a voice for Emily's ears only. "They don't understand."

Emily looked into her mother's gentle face. "Understand what?"

"How much you really love Cooper."

Dinner was a long affair with as much conversation as there was food. By the time the meal was over and the dishes were being scraped, Emily was completely stuffed and terribly drowsy.

The second time she yawned, her mother waved her out of the kitchen. "We have plenty of help with the cleaning up. Go take a little nap."

Emily followed her mother's suggestion and left the noisy kitchen, but she had no intentions of taking a nap. She found her coat and slipped out a back door of the house. The weather had warmed since early morning and though the wind was brisk on her face, it wasn't stinging cold as it could be in New Mexico at this time of year.

Jamming her hands deep into her coat pockets, she ambled out toward the cattle pens, then on toward the stables. When she entered one of the horse barns, she was surprised to find Cooper strolling down the long, sawdust covered alleyway.

The big door creaked as she shut it behind her. Hearing it, Cooper turned, then seeing it was her, he stood and waited until she caught up to him.

As Emily made her way down the alleyway to where he was standing, she couldn't help but notice how sexy he looked today in a collarless white shirt, blue jeans and brown lambskin jacket. But even when Cooper was dressed in flannel shirts, rough-out chaps and muddy boots he managed to stir her senses.

"I thought you were watching the football game with the rest of the men folk," she said.

"I was. But after the score became one-sided I got bored."

She cast him a knowing little grin. "And you got an itch to look at the horses."

He chuckled. "Okay, a little itch." He walked over to the nearest stall and peered over the gate at a paint yearling.

"What a beauty this one is going to be. Does your Aunt Chloe race very many horses now?"

Emily joined him at the stall. "She holds it down to only the bigger futurity races. Which is quite a job in itself. But Chloe would be lost if she wasn't working with her horses."

He looked away from the paint and over the rest of the building. "I don't think I've ever seen such a magnificent ranch. Does it belong solely to Wyatt and Chloe now?"

Emily shook her head. "Even though Chloe and Wyatt are the ones who live here, Mom and Justine are still part owners, too. It's a joint family thing with the sisters and their husbands. Between the six of them, they've turned it into a fine ranch."

"Fine," he said with a grunt of amusement. "This place is more than fine, it's something else. They must be very proud of it."

Sighing, she rested her shoulder against the stall door. "When I first saw this ranch it wasn't anything like it is now. In fact, my mom and her sisters were very close to losing it. I'm sure I've told you about the twins' birth mother setting fire to the place. Hundreds of acres were scorched black. I was only thirteen then, but I still remember it vividly. Those were rough times."

And she was still having rough times, Cooper thought as he looked at her quiet face. It was no wonder she'd grown bitter. After a while a person had to harden themselves just to survive.

"You know, Emily, this—" he made a motion with his hand around the stables "—is what I always wanted the Diamond D to be. When I was much younger, I had all sorts of dreams to make the old Dunn place grow. That's why I left, to earn the money."

For long moments his eyes searched hers. "Why do you think I was such a jerk for wanting more than what I had?"

"Because you were enough for me, Cooper. I wanted to

be enough for you. The rest...if we needed it...would come later.''

If Cooper had known what he knew now, he probably would have made different choices back then. Especially knowing she'd been pregnant with their child. Yet he refused to feel guilty about his wants. They had all been for her. Even now there were so many things he would like to give her. To him, that was a part of loving someone.

"I don't want to argue about this, Emily. I didn't mean to get into any of it in the first place.''

"So why did you? Today of all days, we're supposed to be thankful and happy for what we have.''

Emily was right, Cooper thought. But something about being with Emily's family today had reminded him of all the wonderful things he'd missed. And all those he would never have.

"Tell me, Emily, what do we have? Sure, we have our health. I do thank God for that. We both own a run-down ranch. And you have a baby on the way. But we don't have each other. And we never will.'' His expression bitter, he made a motion with his hand toward the direction of the house. "We'll never have what your parents have. Or your aunts and uncles.''

Fury rose inside Emily and begged her palm to slap his face. "And whose choice was that, Cooper?''

"Yours! You made it ten years ago when you married my brother!''

This time she couldn't stop her hand from flying straight at his head. Seeing it coming, Cooper ducked and snatched a hold on her wrist.

Her breasts heaved as she glared up at him. "I guess it makes you feel better to place all the blame on me and Kenneth. But you need to face reality, Cooper. Your brother is dead and gone. You can't keep blaming him for everything!''

His grip on her wrist tightened while the expression on

his face grew even harder. "Kenneth will never be truly gone from your life. You're having his child. How do you think that makes me feel?"

"Like the selfish bastard you are!" she snapped back at him.

Cooper couldn't think of a time he'd been more furious. Not just at Emily, but with Fate and the unfairness of all that had happened.

"If I'm going to hear you call me that every time I turn around, I might as well act the part," he muttered.

"Act? You don't have to act—"

Her barrage of words were suddenly cut off as he jerked her into his arms. "If that's what you think, then I might as well start taking what I want and quit worrying about the right or wrong of it. You certainly have!"

Her mouth fell open and Cooper didn't hesitate to take advantage. His head swooped down and his lips captured the shocked O of her lips.

To have him kissing her, even in a fit of anger, caught Emily totally off guard. She'd never expected to taste his lips again or feel the hard heat of his body pressed against hers. The sweet treasure of being in his arms again swiftly overrode her anger and in only a matter of seconds she was kissing him back with a passion that stunned him.

Cooper didn't know how he'd gone from being furious one moment to being consumed with desire the next. But somehow it had happened. He couldn't stop his hands from clutching her closer or his tongue from delving deeper into the warm recesses of her giving mouth. She was the only woman he'd ever really needed or wanted. The only woman who could make him forget where they were or why.

The soft nicker of a horse finally broke the heated kiss. His breaths coming rough and rapid, Cooper put her away from him just as the door to the barn opened and Harlan stepped inside.

"There you are," he called cheerfully as he spotted the

two of them. He walked the length of the alleyway until he was within a few steps of them. ''Rose was worried when she didn't find Emily in the bedroom taking a nap.''

Cooper shot her a dry glance before he turned to face her father. ''That's just where she was headed, Harlan.''

''Cooper!''

Ignoring the warning in Emily's voice, he took her by the shoulder and nudged her toward her father. ''Sometimes your daughter has to be reminded of her condition.''

# Chapter Seven

Two weeks into December Cooper decided it was time to head to the livestock auction in Roswell. The fences he'd been working on in the west pasture were patched and the market prices were holding at rock bottom. And Emily was growing larger every day. In less than three months, she'd be giving birth and he'd be saying goodbye to her and the Diamond D. If he was ever going to begin restocking the ranch with cattle, he needed to do it now.

"Okay, I'm ready to go."

Cooper looked up from his coffee cup as Emily entered the kitchen. She was dressed in rust brown corduroy slacks and a matching turtleneck sweater. Both garments were two of those he'd bought for her before Thanksgiving. He knew she considered all the things he'd given as her "dress up" clothes, which she only wore when she went out or someone was coming over for a visit. The reason she was wearing them this morning was all too evident to him.

"You're not going anywhere," he told her.

Smiling confidently, Emily placed her coat on the back

of a chair, then walked over to the coffeepot and poured herself a half cup.

Her chin lifting, she folded her arms beneath her breasts. "Do I look ill? Or just stupid?"

Cooper shook his head. "Neither. And I don't want to argue with you, Emily. So—"

His words broke off as she suddenly rose from her chair and began to pull on her coat. "Then don't. We're wasting time. We need to be there before the auction starts. I don't want to buy cattle I haven't had time to look over first."

Cooper shot to his feet. "*You* don't want to buy? I thought I was the cattle buyer around here."

She gave him a sweet smile as she buttoned her coat. "Maybe you are the money supplier. But I'm the one who's going to be doing the ranching here long after you've hit the road. I think that gives me the right to a little say about things."

She had him over a barrel, Cooper decided.

"Damn it, Emily, if you get sick—"

"I'm not going to get sick." She wrapped a black woolen scarf around her neck as she headed toward the door. "And if I get that tired, I'll make you rent a motel room and we'll drive back tomorrow."

Like hell, she would, Cooper growled to himself. There was no way he'd stay the night in a motel room with Emily. The mere thought of it made him break out in a sweat.

"Okay, okay," he relented and motioned her out the door. "You've won, so let's go. It's already seven and it's an hour and a half drive to Roswell from here."

Halfway into the trip Cooper realized he'd done the right thing by bringing Emily along with him. Each time he glanced over at her, she was smiling and the excitement glowing in her blue eyes told him how much she was enjoying driving across the desert this winter morning.

Several weeks ago, Cooper had come to the conclusion

that Emily had been living a solitary life these past years. She'd been married to Kenneth but from all he could see their life together had not been a happy or prosperous one. He didn't know whose fault that had been. But he got the impression that Emily felt she was the reason things hadn't gone right for them.

"Did you and Kenneth ever go out much?"

The question swung Emily's head back around to him. She didn't know why he still asked her such things about Kenneth and herself. It was like stirring up dead ashes.

"Go out?" she asked. "You mean on special occasions, or what?"

"I mean go out for any reason. Like we're going out today," he explained.

Emily shook her head. "Not much. Kenneth didn't like getting away from the ranch unless it was an absolute necessity. Besides, we never really had the money to do much traveling. Not that Kenneth would have traveled anyway. He never was like you, Cooper. He wasn't an adventurer or gambler."

Surprised by her comment, he glanced at her. "I didn't realize you thought of me in those terms."

Her expression turned dry. "Well, let's face it, Coop, you never were a stay-at-home family man."

Put like that, Cooper supposed he couldn't argue with her. But is that what he'd been doing all these years? he asked himself. Gambling that his riding skills would win him a fortune?

Shrugging, he said, "I guess I was conceited enough to believe I was going to win. I never thought of it as a gamble with my money."

"I was thinking more in terms of your life. Rodeo riders are killed every year. Didn't you—don't you ever think about the danger?"

"I'd be lying if I said it didn't cross my mind once in a while. Especially when a buddy broke his neck or back.

But fear of dying was never on my mind when I climbed onto the back of a bronc.''

It suddenly dawned on him that Emily wasn't thinking about his bronc riding just in terms of the past. Her thoughts were on the future. Could it be that she was actually worried about him going back to the sport? The thought had never entered his mind before now. But perhaps it should have.

"Emily, I'm not going to get killed like Kenneth."

"You think I'm worried about you?" she asked blithely.

"It sounds like it to me."

Emily quickly looked away from him before he could see just how much she really did worry over him. "Well, even though you are…a pain at times, I don't want anything to happen to you."

The soft concern in her voice was very hard for Cooper to resist. But he told himself she would be just as worried over any relative or acquaintance. He couldn't let himself think he was anything special to her. If he did, he was bound to fall into the same heartache she'd dealt him ten years ago.

Emily had been a rancher's daughter and wife all her life. During that time she'd seen plenty of ups and downs in the cattle market, but she could safely say she'd never seen such pitiful cows at prices so rock bottom it was indecent.

"Dear Lord, Cooper, this is enough to send a small rancher racing to the city to hunt for a desk job," Emily told him later that day as they watched another sorry lot of mixed breeds being herded into the auction ring.

He gave her a wry little grin. "Well, they are going cheap."

"I wouldn't have one sorry hoof of them on the Diamond D," she insisted.

Cooper had to admit Emily knew her cattle. So far she

hadn't seen a decent one and so far she'd been dead right. Glancing at his watch, he said, "It's already three o'clock and we haven't bid on one cow. At this rate, the whole trip over here to Roswell is going to be a dry run."

Putting her hands against her back, Emily arched and stretched. The movement didn't go unnoticed by Cooper. For her sake they were going to have to leave soon, whether they'd bought any cattle or not.

"We're not leaving until we get what we want," she promised him.

Cooper lifted his hat and ran a hand through his dark hair. Even though there were a few heaters blowing from the ceiling, it was cold in the bleachers around the auction ring and with nothing to support her back, he knew Emily had to be stiff and exhausted. Yet so far the only complaint he'd heard out of her was the condition of the cattle.

"Emily, it's already going to be late when we get home. You have to be getting tired because I am."

The weary smile she shot at him went straight to Cooper's heart.

"I'm okay," she insisted. "Let's watch a few more sell before we go. Please?"

For the past three weeks, Cooper had kept a safe distance from Emily. If he'd touched her at all it had only been inadvertently. Yet now he found he couldn't stop himself from scooting closer and supporting her back with his arm. "If we don't see a decent cow in thirty minutes, we're outa here. No arguments."

"Okay, a half hour," she agreed, while thinking if he continued to hold her like this, she wouldn't care if they bought any cows. She needed his closeness, his touch, his strength. With each day that passed, she realized that more and more. Yet she also knew she couldn't let herself fall in love with him a second time. He would soon be gone, back to his rodeo life. And she'd be here to go on—without him.

Surprisingly, the next herd of cattle into the auction ring was poor, but well-bred. She and Cooper both agreed with a lot of extra care and decent weather the animals would eventually blossom into a profit.

Unfortunately, a few other cattle buyers sitting around the drafty auction barn had the same idea. But to Emily's surprise, Cooper didn't back down from the bidding until he got the final drop of the gavel on the whole thirty head.

"Do you think you should have spent that much?" she asked him. "Ten thousand dollars is a lot of money."

"I have it."

She frowned at him. "I know you have it. But that's a great deal of funds to invest in something you're…well, come spring you won't even be around to see the cattle."

Emily brought up his leaving often and Cooper figured it must be on her mind. But hell, it was constantly on his mind, too. He kept asking himself how he was ever going to make himself walk away. And if he couldn't, how could he ever find the courage to stay.

"I'll drop in from time to time. And just knowing the ranch is doing better will be enough."

In other words he wouldn't necessarily need to see her. Oh well, she thought resignedly, he'd never professed to love her and she'd never expected him to. But it would be nice to know she would at least be…missed.

More than an hour later Cooper had paid for the cattle and arranged for them to be shipped to the Diamond D. They walked out of the auction barn and discovered snow peppering down from a heavy gray sky.

Emily wrapped her woolen scarf around her neck then reached for Cooper's arm. Now that she'd finally left her seat on the bleachers, she realized she was far more tired than she'd thought.

"I don't want to slip," she explained her reason for holding onto him.

Cooper glanced down at her and suddenly felt like a two-inch heel. What sort of man was he to make Emily think she dare not touch him without a practical reason for it? He didn't want her to think of him as being that cold or distant. He wanted her to lean on him if she needed to. And yet he knew it wasn't quite that simple, either. It really didn't matter why Emily touched him. His reaction to her was always the same. He felt an overwhelming need to love and protect her, to never let her go.

"I really think we should get something to eat before we leave town," he suggested as he helped her into the cab of the pickup truck. "Do you feel up to going to a restaurant?"

She nodded. "I need to eat. I'll try."

Cooper drove them to a downtown steak house where a waitress quickly took their order for T-bones. While they waited for the steaks to be cooked, they ate tossed salad and watched the snow collecting on the street outside.

"Maybe we shouldn't have stopped to eat," Emily said, her fork paused in midair as she gazed out the plate-glass window. "Much more of this and we're going to slip and slide all the way home."

Her face was pale and dark shadows smudged the delicate skin beneath her eyes. The sag of her shoulders told Cooper it was all she could do to remain upright. To put her through the drive back home tonight would be cruel and unnecessary.

"I've decided we should stay here in Roswell tonight."

His announcement jerked her head around. "Stay here? But—"

"You're too tired to make the trip."

"I'm not. Anyway, I can lay down in the seat."

He shook his head. "There's no point in it when we're both tired and the roads are slick. I'll call your dad and ask him to send a wrangler over to feed the livestock for us. We'll drive home in the morning after we eat breakfast."

"Cooper, I know this morning I suggested staying here

overnight, but that was only because I was bargaining with you. You don't have to—''

He put up his hand to ward off anything else she planned to say. "Don't worry about it, Emily. It's no big deal. I've spent ten years in motel rooms. One more night isn't going to hurt me.''

Deciding it wasn't anything to make an issue over, she stabbed a forkful of lettuce and smiled at him. "You know, I can't remember the last time I was away from the ranch overnight. I suppose it was when Mother was sick with the flu and I stayed a couple of nights on the Flying H with her and Dad.'' Shrugging, she gave him another tired smile. "I guess this is the first traveling adventure I've had in a long time.''

The narrowness of Emily's life never ceased to amaze Cooper. There was so much she'd never seen or done, so much she'd lost in the last ten years he'd been away. He wished he could give it all to her. All and more. Yet it terrified him to even think of trying. Maybe eventually he could forgive and forget the fact that she'd married Kenneth rather than waiting for him. But then there would always be the baby to remind him.

"Emily, are you all right?''

Dropping her hand back to the tabletop, she blinked her eyes and gave him the brightest smile she could manage. "I'm fine.''

The expression on his face said he wasn't the least bit convinced. "Something is wrong.''

"I'm just tired.''

A scowl wrinkled his forehead. "I should have never agreed to let you come today. This whole trip has been too much for you.''

Suddenly she wanted to yell, What the hell do you care? What was the point in his show of concern? He didn't care about the baby. He'd already said as much. And as for her, all Emily could figure was he didn't want the nuisance of having a sick woman on his hands. The idea shouldn't bother her, but it did.

"I'm fine," she repeated.

"Are you having second thoughts about the cattle? About us owning the ranch together? Are you trying to tell me you want out?"

Emily didn't know how their conversation had grown into this and she was too weary to try to figure it out. "No! I figure one of these days, you'll want out. And when that time comes I won't be surprised and I won't be worried. It's what I expect of you!"

She was angry with him now, Cooper realized, though he wasn't exactly sure why. He wasn't even sure how they'd arrived on the subject of selling the ranch. But he could see he'd obviously taken a wrong turn with her somewhere.

Reaching across the table, he covered her hand with his. "Emily, don't be upset. In spite of what you think about my staying power, I'm not thinking of selling the ranch or anything of the sort. As far as I'm concerned, I'll never sell it. I just thought you might like to do accounting again because—" He shook his head. "I look at you and I think there's so much more you should have out of life."

"I have everything I need," she told him. Then before she could stop it, her heart silently added, everything but you, Cooper.

Eventually they found a motel on the east edge of town with a Vacancy sign in the window. Emily waited in the truck while Cooper went into the office. A few minutes later he came back with a key dangling from his fingers. One key.

Emily jerked upright in the pickup seat. "You only rented one room?"

"We were damn lucky to get the one. From what the manager of this place told me, every motel in town is full.

There's some sort of Christmas festival going on in town over the weekend.''

Well, surely there would be two beds, Emily assured herself. But once they were inside the room, she found herself staring at the one double bed as if it were a jail cell. What had Cooper been thinking? He didn't want to share a bed with her!

"What's the matter now?" Cooper asked, glancing over his shoulder at her as he bolted the door lock.

Her eyes wide, she looked around at him. "I'm just wondering which one of us gets the bed."

"You do, of course. There's a chair over there in the corner or I'll get on the floor."

Emily wasn't about to let either of those things happen, but she kept it to herself. She was too tired to argue with him at this point. Later after she'd rested a few minutes, she'd make him see that she wasn't planning to pounce on him. He would be perfectly safe lying beside her on the mattress.

After making use of the bathroom, Emily sat down on the edge of the bed and pulled off her snow boots. While she'd been out of the room, Cooper had turned on the small television situated on a nearby dresser. Presently a local weatherman was on the screen, predicting at least three to four more inches of snow before the night was over.

"Well, at least we got what we came after," she commented as she sat on top of the covers.

Seeing she still had her coat on, Cooper crossed the room to a wall furnace and turned it as high as it would go.

"Yeah, we got the cattle," he agreed. He came back over to the bed and sat down at the head where a phone was located. Once he had Harlan on the other end of the line, he briefly explained the situation, then assured him they would be back home on the Diamond D tomorrow.

After Cooper hung up, Emily asked, "Is he going to send a man over to feed for us?"

"He promised he would."

She sighed with relief. "Did he say whether it was snowing there?"

"Like a blizzard. He's glad we're not trying to drive home in it."

The heat was beginning to fill the room. Emily pulled off her coat and hung it on a rack fastened to the wall. Cooper left his seat on the bed and wandered restlessly over to the windows.

Pulling back the curtain a fraction, he peered out at the parking lot. Snow was falling thick and fast, collecting on the shrubs and parked vehicles. It was a scene he'd seen a thousand times over in a countless number of towns and cities. Yet tonight was nothing like those he'd spent traveling on the road. Emily was with him. She gave his being here meaning and purpose.

"What are you looking at?" she asked after a moment.

He glanced over at the bed where she was stretched out on her back, her head cushioned with a pillow. "Nothing. Just the snow."

"Come over here and sit down," she invited. She knew he had to be tired and the only chair in the room was built for decorative purposes, not for comfort.

"I've been sitting all evening. I need to stand up."

"Don't be silly. I'm not going to bite you."

"I wasn't worried that you were," he said, then letting the curtain drop, he walked over to the bed and took a seat on the opposite side from her. "Would you like for me to go get you something else to eat? It's a long time until bedtime."

She groaned. "I couldn't eat another bite of anything." Her eyes swiveled over to him. "But if you want to go out, don't worry about me. I'll be fine."

He shook his head. "I don't need to go out." Everything he wanted was right here, he thought. That was the whole problem. Then he quickly told himself he was being foolish. He'd lived in the same house with Emily now for nearly three months and he'd managed to keep a grip on himself. Just because they were cooped up in a small room together didn't make things any different. She was the same Emily here as she was there. If he could resist her there, he could do it here.

"You needn't look so worried, Cooper. I'm not going to try to seduce you." With a forced little laugh, she patted the mound of her stomach. "I'm hardly in form for it. I'm sure your taste runs to slim young cowgirls."

Cooper would have thought so, too. He'd certainly seen a lot of them down through the years. And without any conceit on his part, he'd had more than a few make themselves available to him. Yet surprisingly, none of those women had looked as beautiful as Emily did to him at this moment. Even with her swollen belly and fatigue painting shadows on her face, she was the most desirable woman he'd ever seen. How could that be? How could he still want her so badly? He'd loved her. He'd planned on making her his wife. Yet she'd turned to Kenneth while he'd been away. A man shouldn't want a woman who could forget him that easily, he thought. But he couldn't seem to stop himself no matter how hard he fought it.

"Don't be flip, Emily. It isn't fair to either of us."

Struck by his words, she studied him for long moments. His face was too stoic to read, yet one thing was obviously clear. He wished he was anywhere but here with her. The knowledge cut her deep.

"Oh, Cooper, don't be ridiculous. I'm not young anymore and neither are you. We don't have to put up a pretense with each other."

His gray eyes focused on her face. "Pretense?"

"Yes," she answered. Turning onto her side, she propped her head on her bent elbow. As her eyes surveyed his face, she said, "I'm not blind. Right now you're thinking if you lie down here beside me something will happen between us.''

"Something?"

"Yes. You and me. As we were in the Bar M stables Thanksgiving Day.'' She laughed, though the sound was more like a strangled gurgle in her throat than one of amusement. "Well, I'm telling you not to worry. You got the message over to me loud and clear that day. You don't want me. You have no intentions of starting any sort of relationship with me. I under—''

"Emily, I wish you wouldn't talk this way,'' he interrupted sharply.

"Why? Because hearing the truth bothers you?''

His features twisted into something like a snarl. "Truth! You don't know the truth. If you did, you wouldn't be '' He broke off with a resigned shake of his head. "Forget it! I'm going to find a movie on TV and after we watch it, we're going to sleep. I'm not going to seduce you and you're not going to seduce me. And neither of us will feel guilty in the morning!''

Emily could have told him it wouldn't make her feel a bit guilty if she seduced him. She was a woman after all, with a woman's needs. Would it be so wrong to take a few minutes pleasure in his arms? she asked herself. But the rational part of her knew making love with Cooper would only make it harder to say goodbye.

The pain was excruciating. It started in her back and radiated around to her sides, then spread over her entire stomach. Yet as terrible as the pain was the fear was far worse. No matter where she looked or turned there was no one there to help her. What was she going to do? Where was Cooper and why had he left her alone?

"Emily, wake up!''

Tortured groans slipped past her parted lips as her head twisted back and forth on the pillow.

"Emily! It's Cooper. Are you ill?"

His voice penetrated her sleep-induced terror. Slowly she opened her eyes. The room was dark but she could make out the dim outline on his face hovering above hers.

"Oh God. Oh thank God it was only a dream," she whispered, then clutching his shoulders, she buried her face in the side of his neck.

Tremors shook the length of her body and Cooper instinctively slid his arms around her and gathered her close to him. "Are you sure you were only dreaming? You're not hurting anywhere?"

Her head moved back and forth against him. "I'm not hurting. I'm shaking because I was so scared." She tilted her head back in an effort to see his face. Her voice quivered as she began to speak again. "I dreamed I was back home on the ranch and I'd gone into labor...but you had left...there was no one around to help me. The pain was splitting me apart and I didn't know what to do."

Even though Cooper knew it was only a dream and not real pain that had woken her, he still wanted to comfort her, to reassure her that she wasn't alone.

"Emily, you know I'm not going to leave until the baby is safely born."

"You might change your mind and go before then," she whispered.

"I won't. I promise."

But he would leave later. She and the baby would truly be alone then. Oh, her parents would be glad to hire a live-in housekeeper to stay with her. But Emily didn't want hired companionship. She wanted a family. A husband and a father for her baby. She wanted Cooper to be those things!

Yet, he'd told her over and over he wasn't a family man. She needed to accept that and forget him once and for all. So why couldn't she?

Because her heart loved him. It couldn't let him go. The

answers tore through her with shocking clarity as his hand stroked the back of her hair and his face nuzzled the side of her head.

"Emily, right now you think you want me to hang around. But you'll feel differently once the baby is born. Your whole life is going to change. You won't need me."

Dear Lord, did he honestly think that? Or did thinking it simply make him feel better about leaving?

"Cooper, earlier tonight you said I didn't know the truth. I don't know what you meant by that, but—"

Suddenly his hands were framing her face. With his thumbs locked beneath her cheekbones, his eyes bored mercilessly into hers. "It means I'm sick of you taunting me. Do you think I'm heartless? Do you think I don't need the same things you need?"

Everything inside her went still as his questions spun through her mind. "No—you don't need me. Or this baby growing inside me!"

"Damn you, Emily! You—" He didn't finish. He couldn't. Too much need and anger and frustration was welling up inside him. Before he could stop himself, his lips were fastened roughly to hers.

Whimpering at the unexpected onslaught, Emily tried to twist her head away. But the viselike grip of his hands refused her any slack. It wasn't until his lips had hungrily punished hers that he finally lifted his head and drew in a ragged breath.

"Do you think all those years away cured me of you?" he flung at her. "Do you think I've forgotten what it was like to have you in my arms? To make love to you?"

"Yes! I think you quickly forgot me and your home!"

A feral smile spread his lips, making his white teeth gleam in the darkness. At that moment Emily thought of him as a lone wolf, angrily baring his teeth to keep anyone or thing from entering his territory.

The pads of his fingers moved over her swollen lips. "I

haven't forgotten anything about you, Emily. Not this. Or this." His hand slid to the hard mound of her breast, then lower still to the intimate V between her thighs. "Or this," he added hoarsely. "And I thought you loved me back then. But hell, I can see now that you didn't even know me! When I got the news you'd married Kenneth it literally made me sick. A part of me died and I'll never get it back."

He rolled away from her then and with tortured eyes Emily watched him struggle to bring his angry breaths back to normal.

"You hate me," she said with certain finality.

"Hate you?" He laughed harshly. "Right now I want you like hell. But I won't have you. You took that right away from me years ago."

So he was never going to forgive her for marrying Kenneth. Somehow she'd known he couldn't. Or wouldn't. Deep down inside her she just hadn't wanted to accept it.

Tears were burning her throat, scalding the back of her eyes, but pride managed to keep them at bay. "So why do you care if I'm cold or tired or hurting? What the hell difference does it make to you if I'm alone on the ranch when I go into labor?"

His expression unmoving, he looked at her. "One Dunn woman already lost her life in childbirth. I don't want two on my hands."

So that was it, Emily thought sickly. His show of concern wasn't really for her at all. It was an atonement of sorts for his mother's death. He wasn't even thinking of the miscarriage she suffered with his child.

Her chest heavy with pain, she turned away from him and prayed for sleep to come.

# Chapter Eight

"No, Mother," Emily said into the phone. "I don't want Daddy to go to the trouble of bringing a tree all the way over here. He has enough to do as it is."

"But, darling, it's Christmas! You always put up a tree," Rose argued with her daughter.

Emily's gaze traveled around the living room of the old ranch house. For the past week she'd slowly dug out decorations from the closet. The fireplace mantel was now graced with pinecones, red candles and gold tinsel. A papier-mâché reindeer and Santa Claus sat on the coffee table. On a table near the windows, she'd arranged a small nativity scene her parents had given her as a gift many years ago.

The ranch house looked a little more like Christmas, but it didn't feel like the season of love and goodwill to Emily. Since their trip to Roswell a little over a week ago, Cooper had become a polite stranger to her. He was eating and sleeping under the same roof as she, but that was where it began and ended. He talked to her only when it was necessary or when she forced him to and even then he kept their conversations brief and to the point.

"I know it's nearly Christmas and I don't have a tree," Emily spoke into the phone. "But I have most of my decorations out. And besides, it's just me and Cooper here and he couldn't care less."

Picking up the antipathy in her daughter's voice, Rose said gently, "But you care. That's the whole point. And I want this Christmas to be special for you."

How could it be special? Emily wondered. Sometime during the past few months, she'd allowed herself to do the unthinkable. She'd fallen in love with Cooper all over again. Since the realization had struck her that night in Roswell, it was all she could think about. She was headed for a terrible heartache and she didn't have a clue as to how to stop it.

"Oh, Mother," she said with a sigh, "I don't think I can ever remember a Christmas—so bleak. I almost wished it were over because I—well, I just wished it were over."

"Emily!" Rose scolded softly. "You should be ashamed. You have a healthy baby growing inside you. There's no greater gift than that. And you've wanted a child for so long."

Emily felt a desperate urge to cry but she swallowed her tears. She didn't want to upset her mother. Rose probably wouldn't understand, any more than Emily, why she felt so melancholy. After all, it wasn't like she'd ever expected Cooper to love her. She'd had ten years to accept that he didn't. Why should it be bothering her so now?

"You're right, Mother. I should be ashamed and I am. This baby means everything to me. Without it...I don't know if I could go on." A sad smile tilting the corners of her lips, she pressed her hand against the persistent kick against her stomach. "I only wish that—"

"You only wish things could be different with you and Cooper. Aren't I right?"

Sighing, she leaned up and pushed aside the antique lace curtain. It was getting dusky outside and she hadn't yet heard Cooper come in. "Yes. I hate to admit it, Mom. Especially—" She broke off suddenly as her eyes focused on the gray horse and rider in the distance. "Oh my Lord, I can't believe it!"

"What is it, Emily? Has something happened to you?" Rose very nearly shouted when Emily failed to say more.

"It's—Cooper and he has a tree! I'll call you back later, Mother!"

By the time Emily had jerked on a pair of boots and a coat, Cooper had reached the backyard. She raced down the steps and out to where he'd dismounted the gray and was slipping the loop of his lariat from the tree trunk.

"Where ever did you find it? You have to ride miles to the south to find ponderosa on this place!"

Cooper rolled up the lariat and tossed the stiff coils over the saddle horn. A quick glance at Emily's face told him he'd never seen her looking so excited. She was practically dancing on her toes.

"I know."

Stepping closer, she leaned down and fingered the prickly green needles. "It smells wonderful!" She turned back to him. "You rode all that way? Just for a tree?"

Her expression said he'd shocked her. Cooper had to admit he'd surprised himself by going to such lengths to get a Christmas tree. He hadn't intended to. Considering they weren't a couple who could take joy in sharing holiday traditions, he'd figured it would be better to let the holiday pass without making a fuss. But day after day this week, he'd watched Emily dragging out those damn decorations, trying to give the old homestead a little holiday cheer. He couldn't bear to be a scrooge when she seemed content to make do with so little.

"When your dad was here yesterday I asked him if you usually put up a tree." Shrugging, he glanced back at the spindly pine. "I'd forgotten just how few trees are on this ranch. I had to drag it for such a long way, it's probably bald on the backside."

Emily wouldn't have cared if it was nothing but bare branches. Cooper *was* thinking about Christmas! Suddenly the approaching holidays didn't seem gloomy at all!

"If you'd driven into Ruidoso and bought the most beautiful blue spruce you could find, I wouldn't have liked it any better."

She was reading too much into it. Just as Cooper had been afraid she would. But this was the season for giving. And a tree was such a simple thing. Not like a jewel or a scent, or even a kiss.

Cooper stood the pine up on its trunk and measured the height against his own. It towered at least three feet above the crown of his gray hat. "Looks like it will fit in the living room without having to cut any more off the trunk."

"Oh, it will!" she exclaimed, then her face puckered as she remembered something. "But, Cooper, the stand is broken. What are we going to put it in? To stay green it will need to be watered."

He thought for a moment. "There's a galvanized foot tub in the feed room. I'll fill it full of soil and rocks."

"I'll go find it." Emily took one step toward the barn only to have Cooper grab her by the upper arm.

"I'll get the tub," he insisted. "You go back in the house and find the decorations for the tree. You do have some, don't you?"

"Yes," she answered with an eager nod. "I'll get them out and we can decorate after supper."

*We?* Cooper had no intentions of helping her drape garland and icicles, but he said nothing. The smile on her face made it impossible for him to burst her bubble right now.

More than an hour later after the two of them had eaten stew and apple cobbler, Cooper planted the tree in the galvanized tub and pulled the whole thing into the living room to the spot Emily had chosen. However, as soon as he satisfied himself the tree was going to remain upright and steady, he went back to the kitchen for a second cup of coffee.

Emily wasn't surprised by his quick exit and she did her best not to let it bother her. She told herself he'd gone to a lot of trouble of getting the tree. That was far more than she'd ever expected from him.

From a large box of decorations, she dug out a half dozen strings of twinkling lights and painstakingly untangled them. Afterward, she plugged them in a nearby socket to make sure they were all still working.

Happy to see the bulbs were burning, she carried the lights over to the tree and began working them around the bottom branches. Everything went fine until she was down to the last two strands of lights and her arms were at least three feet too short to reach the top branches. What was she going to do? Go ask Cooper for help? No. She wasn't going to force him into sharing this Christmas ritual with her. She'd rather do it herself.

Glancing around the room, Emily spotted a wooden straight-back chair that would work nicely as a step stool. She pushed it over to the tree and climbed carefully onto the seat.

"What in hell do you think you're doing?" Cooper asked harshly as he suddenly walked back into the room.

Having grown accustomed to his unexpected outbursts, she glanced calmly over her shoulder. "I'm putting the rest of the lights on the tree," she said with exaggerated patience. "I couldn't reach the top."

Crossing the space of the room in three long strides, Cooper took hold of her hand. "That's too bad. Because you're getting out of that chair right now."

She rolled her eyes with frustration. "Cooper, I always put the lights on. You have to do them just right to make the tree look pretty."

"You might always make them look pretty, but not this year. Now come on. Get down." He tugged on her hand and with a groan of resignation she stepped off the chair and safely onto the floor.

"Now what am I going to do?"

He took the chair and placed it a couple of feet away from the tree. "Sit here and drink this." He handed her the remainder of his coffee. "And tell me what to do. I don' know anything about decorating a Christmas tree, but I'l try."

Emily knew he didn't want to string Christmas lights but he was willing to try just to keep her out of the chair. Was it really thoughts of his mother that made him this way with her? she asked herself for the thousandth time. He seemed so intent on keeping her safe and healthy, i almost made her believe he actually cared about her and possibly even the baby. But in the next breath, she told herself she was crazy to think such things. Cooper Dunn didn't love her. She wasn't really sure he'd ever loved any one or that he even knew how.

"There's nothing to tell. Just wrap the cord in and ou around the branches," she instructed him. "Like those I've already put at the bottom."

Cooper examined the lights she'd already placed on the tree, then went to work with two remaining strands. While he awkwardly wrapped and poked the electrical wire, Emily sipped his coffee and watched.

"Have you never decorated a Christmas tree before Cooper?" she asked after a moment.

He shook his head. "As long as I lived here we never had a tree in this house."

Kenneth had already told her as much and Emily figured that's how things had always been in the Dunn house with out a mother around and a father as hard as rawhide. She hated to think what it had been like for him growing up with a father who had never considered his wants or needs

And a brother who hadn't had enough gumption or love to stand up for him.

"What about the woman with the little boy? Didn't she celebrate Christmas?"

Nonplussed, he glanced over his shoulder at her. "What woman?"

Had there been that many? With a frown of disgust, she said, "The woman you had a...relationship with."

Why would Emily remember something like that, Cooper wondered, when he could barely remember it himself. "I...wasn't around her during the holidays," he answered with faint annoyance.

"Oh. I guess not with the National Finals Rodeo always being in December," she said thoughtfully.

With a little snort, he turned back to the tree and the lights. "No. The Finals weren't the reason. I...we just no longer had any connection with each other. But if I were guessing, I'm sure she had a Christmas tree and the whole nine yards. She would do anything for that little boy of hers."

"Most mothers would," she told him, then realized he could hardly know about such things. He'd never had a mother's love or soft touch to comfort him or even spoil him from time to time.

"Yeah," he said, "But this child was spoiled rotten. After a few hours with him it was easy for me to swear off women and children."

Emily's baby suddenly gave a rapid succession of kicks as though it could hear Cooper's negative remarks. Yet Emily herself wasn't surprised by his attitude. Basically he'd told her all this before and after three months of living with the man she could plainly see he had no desire to be a husband and a father. Maybe his feelings did partly stem from his bad relationship with his own father and the experience he'd had with his girlfriend's spoiled child. But in the innermost part of her, Emily knew his problem was really with her and Kenneth. He felt betrayed by the both of them. And the fact that she'd lost his baby only made him resent this one even more.

Rising from the chair, she placed the empty cup on a nearby end table and picked up a small box of glass ornaments. As she hung the brightly colored balls from branch to branch, Cooper glanced curiously down at her.

"Aren't you going to give me a long lecture about being heartless and twisted? Aren't you going to tell me how much I'm missing in life by not having a family?"

Not bothering to look up at him, she said, "No, Cooper, I've learned my opinion or feelings leave about as much impression on you as a pile of horse biscuits. You're going to do what you want to do and to hell with anyone else."

He'd never heard her talk this way. As though he were a hopeless cause and could never be reformed. Not that Cooper needed or wanted to be reformed. But up until their cattle buying trip to Roswell a few days ago, he'd held the suspicion she was still holding out hopes he would stay on the Diamond D with her after the baby was born.

But now, well, it was like she'd given up on him and accepted that the two of them were never going to be truly together. The knowledge should have pleased Cooper. After all, it was damn hard to resist her under any circumstances. Knowing she'd wanted him had made it hard as hell to turn his back on her. Yet at some point her feelings toward him had obviously changed. So why wasn't he a happy man?

Cooper finished draping the lights on the top part of the tree and climbed down from the chair with the intention to leave the room and let Emily finish on her own. It was just an old tree. Nothing to make a big deal over, he told himself. Yet as he stood to one side, watching her place each ornament in its own special spot, he discovered he didn't really want to leave. The smell, the colors, the pleasure on Emily's face beckoned him to stay and see what he'd been missing all these years.

"Would you like to put these on?" She handed him a small box of painted wooden angels, soldiers, Santas and reindeer.

"I wouldn't know where," he told her.

"It doesn't matter. Just put them where you think they look best."

Chuckling, he lifted up one of the reindeers and hung it on the pine branch nearest to him. "This is sorta silly, don't you think? We're grown-ups. We know there isn't going to be a Santa come down through the chimney and leave us gifts under the tree."

Emily suddenly thought of the baby growing inside her and these past three months she'd had with Cooper. Though he would soon be going, she knew the weeks he'd spent on the ranch was time with him she'd never expected to have. And she knew she'd already been given her gifts.

"Who knows, Cooper, maybe there is a Santa Claus, after all."

Cooper was relieved when the holidays were finally over. It was a time for families and Cooper didn't have a family. Oh, Emily's relatives had included him in all the festivities and for her sake he'd went along to all of them. But throughout all the partying he'd felt as if he were standing on the outside of the fence looking in through the barbed wire.

At least now he could get on with his work on the ranch. And there were still plenty of things to be done. The Diamond D was a long way from being the ranch he wanted it to be. But he had to admit it was greatly improved from when he'd first arrived back in October. He'd done an enormous amount of carpentry work on the barn and connecting corrals. The outlying boundary fences were all standing straight and tall again and there were thirty more head of mama cows on the place than there had been before. Not that thirty was a great lot, but it was a start at improving the herd.

This past week Cooper had received several calls from his traveling buddies. Each of them asking the same questions. What was he doing and when was he coming back to rodeo? Several of the biggest performances of the year would be coming up in the next few weeks of February. If he missed them, he'd be running at the back of the pack.

There really hadn't been any need for his friends to remind him. Cooper knew the road schedule and what he had to do to stay in the running. But he wasn't at all sure he wanted to go back to that life. For ten years he'd traveled like a freight train out of control. His body had been whipped and jerked and trampled by hundreds of bucking horses. At night he'd gone to bed with pain and the next morning he'd risen with it. He was getting too old for the life, or maybe the life had grown old to him. Whatever the case, since he'd been here on the Diamond D with Emily, he'd come to realize just how sweet it was to call a spot of ground your own. Yet he couldn't stay here. Even though he'd come to need the ranch and Emily, he couldn't be what she needed him to be.

As best as the doctor could tell, she was only six weeks away from her due time. Cooper had started counting the days, marking them off in his mind as an inmate waiting for his execution. Now he could only look to the end as a blessed relief.

The rattle of a pickup crossing the cattle guard leading into the yard lifted Cooper out of his thoughts. Turning, he saw Emily's father, Harlan, parking at the back of the house.

Tossing the feed sack onto the bed of the old work truck, he walked over to greet the man.

"Looks like you've brought some things for Emily's nursery," he said to the older man as he spotted the baby furniture in the bed of the truck.

Harlan grinned as though he were the proud papa rather than just the grandpa. "It's getting about that time and Rose can't wait to help Emily get the nursery fixed up. I don't know who's more excited about this baby coming, Emily or her mother. 'Course her aunts and cousins are right there in the running, too."

Cooper gave the other man a polite smile. "Yes. I guess it will be a big occasion for your family."

"That it will be," Harlan agreed. He walked to the back of the truck and let down the tailgate. "But I figure it will be just as special for you, too, Cooper."

Cooper tried not to look as blank as he felt. "Why do you say that? Kenneth is gone, he won't be here to see his child."

Harlan quickly shook his head. "I wasn't thinking about Kenneth. I was thinking about you. As far as I know you're the only Dunn left in these parts."

Cooper jammed his hands deep into the pockets of his sheepskin coat. The day had been cold and cloudy and there appeared to be snow falling over toward the Capitan mountains. He figured it would reach the Diamond D within the hour.

"I believe I'm the only Dunn left in this part of New Mexico," Cooper told him.

Harlan slapped him kindly on the shoulder. "Well, you won't be the only Dunn around here for much longer. That ought to make you feel proud."

Emily's baby would be a Dunn. But it would never be his, Cooper thought. Surely Harlan could see how that made him feel. He'd wanted Emily to have *his* child. Not Kenneth's. Not anybody's but *his*.

His insides raw with regret, Cooper did his best to smile and nod. "Well, it looks like it's going to snow. I better help you get these things in."

The sound of the two men's boots on the living-room tile woke Emily from her sleep. As soon as her eyes focused on Cooper and Harlan, she jerked upright as though she'd been caught stealing cookies.

"Emily, are you not feeling well?" Cooper asked with a worried frown, then before she could answer, he strode over and put his palm to her forehead.

With a wry little grin Emily glanced from Cooper over to her father. "He's never caught me napping," she explained.

Harlan stepped closer. "You are feeling okay, aren't you, honey?"

Cooper finally dropped his hand away from her brow. Emily rose from the couch and went to kiss her father's cheeks. "I'm fine," she assured him. "Just a little tired. I get that way pretty often these days."

Harlan patted her shoulder. "Then I picked a bad time to surprise you."

"Surprise?" She glanced at Cooper, who had suddenly taken an unusually keen interest in the fire burning in the fireplace. Looking back to her father she asked, "What is it? Don't tell me you've bought me another Appaloosa. Cooper doesn't want me to ride the one I've got."

Harlan laughed. "No. It isn't another horse. Come on out to the back of the house and I'll show you."

Emily quickly grabbed her coat from the closet and followed the two men outside. The moment her eyes spotted the baby furniture, she squealed with delight.

"Daddy! What have you done? Aunt Chloe and Justine were planning on buying the baby's furniture."

Harlan laughed again. "Well, just wait till they find out their brother-in-law beat them to it."

Emily hurried off the porch and out to the pickup. There was a white wooden crib, a matching chest and dressing table and a cradle that rocked at the slightest touch.

She was so overwhelmed by the gifts, tears brimmed over her lashes and fell onto her cheeks.

"It's so...oh, Daddy, how did you know just what I wanted?"

Harlan seemed to understand and even expect his daughter's display of emotion. Smiling gently, he hugged her to him and said, "That's what daddies are for, honey."

*That's what daddies are for.* The words lingered in Cooper's mind as he watched Harlan with his daughter. The man knew all about being a father. He knew how to love and laugh and scold and advise and do all the right things for his children at just the right time. Emily was very lucky to have him. And she would be even luckier if she could find a man so wise and strong to father her coming child. But it couldn't be him. He didn't know how to be like Harlan or even if he had that sort of love and understanding inside him.

In a matter of moments snow began to fall so Cooper and Harlan hurriedly carried the crib, chest and dresser into the house and set it up in the empty bedroom Emily planned to use as a nursery.

"What about this?" Harlan asked as they carried the cradle down the hallway.

"Oh, I want that in my bedroom," Emily answered quickly. "Right by my bed. This little guy isn't going to sleep in a room by himself until he's a whole lot bigger."

"Listen at her," Harlan laughed as he and Cooper placed the cradle at the side of Emily's bed. "He this and he that. What is she going to do if it turns out to be a timid little girl?"

Emily laughed, even though she noticed there wasn't so much as a smile on Cooper's face. "If he turns out to be a she, I'll teach her to ride and rope and shoot better than either one of you."

Harlan chuckled. "I bet you will at that."

Awkwardly clearing his throat, Cooper made his way toward the door. "If you two will excuse me, I'd better get on back to my feeding."

Father and daughter turned to look at him.

"Thanks for your help, Cooper," she told him.

"Do you need me to give you a hand? I don't have to be back to the Flying H for a little while," Harlan told him.

Cooper was touched by the older man's offer. Harlan seemed to genuinely like him, or maybe he simply liked that Cooper was making the ranch a much better place for his daughter. Either way, Cooper was glad Emily's father didn't hold it against him for leaving Lincoln county all those years ago.

"Thanks, Harlan, but you stay and visit with Emily. I'll be finished before dark."

Cooper left the house and for several long minutes Harlan watched his daughter examine the baby cradle, but eventually the words on his mind were impossible to hold back.

"Honey, you know I've never been one to press into your private life. Even though there's been some times down through the years I wanted to drive over here and take you away from this place, I stopped myself. I knew you were a grown woman and I couldn't make choices for you. But I'm going to be frank with you now. Kenneth was a damn sorry husband."

Slowly Emily turned away from the cradle to see her father standing on the other side of the bedroom, gazing out the window.

"My word, Daddy, why are you saying something like that now? Kenneth is gone."

Harlan sighed, as though he half regretted saying anything. "I know. But I...felt like I should tell you what I thought. Especially now that his brother is here. I just...don't want you making any more mistakes."

"Mistakes?" Her brows arched. "Cooper isn't—"

"I know how you feel about the man. I can see it all over your face."

With an annoyed shake of her head, she said, "I wasn't

aware I looked like a lovesick puppy. I guess everyone is getting a good laugh out of me.''

Harlan left the window and walked over to his daughter. Placing a hand on her shoulder, he said, ''There's nothing funny about loving someone, darling. It's a precious gift. I want to make sure you don't waste it this time.''

Her eyes lifted to his gentle gaze and suddenly her heart was breaking with pain. ''Waste it? Oh, Daddy, if you think—'' She drew in a ragged breath and did her best to go on, ''I'm not planning on marrying Cooper.''

''Why not?''

She gasped. ''Why not? I thought…isn't that what you've been trying to say, that you think I'd be making a mistake if I married Cooper?''

''Hell no! I think you'd be making a mistake if you didn't.''

Her mouth fell open as she stared at him. ''But I thought— Mother said you were pretty upset with Cooper all those years ago when he left and—''

''Damn right I was upset then,'' Harlan interrupted. ''I could see how hurt you were. But that's in the past and being a man I can understand the choices Cooper was forced to make. He'd been excluded from this place by his own family—''

''Kenneth loved Cooper. He didn't run him off the ranch,'' Emily said pointedly.

Harlan let out a sarcastic laugh. ''He might as well have. He didn't share the running of this ranch with Cooper or encourage him to make the place his home, too.''

Emily opened her mouth to protest, but her father didn't give her the chance.

''Think about it, Emily. The only thing Kenneth ever did was encourage his brother to hit the road.''

''But that was because…Kenneth knew how good Cooper was at riding broncs. He encouraged him to make a career of it.''

A twisted smile on his face, her father said, "And why do you think that was? Hell, Emily, Kenneth wasn't thinking about Cooper. He was thinking about himself."

Stunned by this new picture her father was painting, Emily turned and walked over to the bed she'd once shared with Kenneth Dunn. Staring at the quilted coverlet, she began to see so many things in the past she'd merely accepted without question. And the awful truth was so sickening, so painful she wanted to lie down and weep until there was nothing left inside her.

"Daddy, do you think—" Eager now to understand what she hadn't known, Emily whirled around and hurried back to her father. "Do you really think Kenneth deliberately tried to get Cooper away from here?"

He nodded and she clutched his big arms as an unfamiliar weakness hit her knees.

"Emily, I first met the Dunns right after we moved out here to New Mexico when you were only a small child. I watched both sons grow up, so I knew them. Kenneth was a subtle manipulator. Both with his father and his brother. He knew you and Cooper were involved, but he wanted you for himself."

Yes, Kenneth had known she and Cooper had been lovers. For a brief time he'd known she was carrying Cooper's child. Yet he hadn't tried to contact his brother about her condition or encourage him to come back home. Instead he'd pressed her to forget Cooper and marry him instead.

Now that Emily thought about it, down through the years Kenneth had always reacted in a jealous way whenever Cooper's name had come up. At the time, she'd taken his behavior as a husband unable to deal with his wife's past. But maybe that wasn't all his reaction had been. More than likely he'd felt guilty about stealing his brother's sweetheart, she thought sickly.

"Daddy...all this is so—" She broke off and pressed her fingers against her forehead. "Why didn't you tell me this years ago? When Cooper left and I turned to Kenneth?''

Harlan shook his head. ''Emily, I tried in many ways to tell you Kenneth wasn't all that he appeared to be. But you were young and you only heard what you wanted to hear. Then later after you married Kenneth, I knew I had to respect your decision and not interfere in your marriage. The last thing I wanted to do was cause trouble between the two of you. But I guess there was always trouble between the two of you anyway.''

And the trouble had been Cooper, Emily thought. Standing between them like a ghost. She hadn't been able to stop loving him and Kenneth had— ''Oh God,'' she whispered, then spearing her fingers through her hair she shoved the thick mass away from her face. ''When I think of all the awful things I've said to Cooper…it crushes me. And all those years I felt guilty. Damn it all, *I* felt guilty!''

Her eyes widened with sudden dawning and she grabbed her father's forearms a second time. ''Daddy, I…all this time I felt I was responsible for Kenneth's drinking. But now I believe the man was riddled with guilt. He not only pushed his brother out of his home, he also stole the woman he loved. The whole thing must have been eating him until the day he died.''

Harlan nodded grimly. ''I'm sure it was,'' Harlan agreed. ''So now what? Cooper is here and you've got a chance to make things up to him.''

The revelation of the last few minutes had lifted a heavy dark cloak from Emily's shoulders. Now she could clearly see why Kenneth had never turned out to be the husband she'd thought he would be. And Cooper, oh Lord how she'd wronged him. How she'd hurt him. But it hadn't been intentional. When he'd left New Mexico she'd honestly believed he didn't want to marry her or make a home with her. And now…it was too late.

"Oh, Dad, I'm afraid…too much has happened for that. Cooper doesn't want anything from me."

"Bull!" Harlan scoffed. "The man is here, isn't he? I don't figure he came back to Lincoln county for his health or a run-down ranch."

Groaning at the unfairness of it all, she turned away from her father and walked back over to the cradle. With a gentle finger she pushed the tiny bed into motion. God willing, her baby would soon sleep here beside her. She would love it fiercely. She already did. Why couldn't Cooper love it, too? Because it was Kenneth's child? Or because it was hers?

"Cooper tried to explain to me that a man has to have something of his own. I can understand a little better now what he meant by that and why…he says he has to leave after the baby is born."

"Leave!" Harlan practically shouted, then added several choice curse words when Emily nodded. "What the hell is the man leaving for? Everything he ever wanted is here."

Emily wasn't at all sure about that. But she was certain he didn't want what was here now. Especially her and the baby.

"He still thinks of me as Kenneth's wife." She placed her hands on her bulging middle. "And this is Kenneth's child. He doesn't want any part of us. And I guess…I can't blame him."

"Oh, Emily." Seeing the misery on his daughter's face, he went to her and pulled her close against his chest. "If that's the way things are, why are you staying here? Why don't you sell this damn place and come back home to the Flying H? Your mother and I would love having you and the baby in the house with us."

Emily knew her father wasn't just mouthing an invitation because he thought he ought to. He truly would enjoy having her at home. He was that kind of man. A man who would love and nurture his family for the rest of his life.

She tilted her head back and looked up at him. "It's comforting to know you and Mother feel that way. Especially with Ethan home now, too. But I...don't want to sell my part of the Diamond D. It was built by a Dunn more than a hundred years ago and it's been in the family ever since. The ranch is a legacy to my unborn child."

Harlan quietly studied the determination on her face. "Your child might grow up to be a doctor or scientist, anything but a rancher. Then what? You've already put ten years of your life into this place, how much more are you going to invest?"

As she considered his question, a wan smile tilted her lips. With or without Cooper, she knew this was where she belonged and where she would stay.

"Whatever my child decides to do is entirely up to him. But I want to be able to give him a choice. I don't want him, or her, to ever go through what Cooper has gone through."

Harlan gently smoothed a hand over the crown of her hair. "You know, I think me and your mother raised a hell of a daughter."

Emily blinked at the moisture stinging her eyes. "I'm not so sure about that. I've made some bad choices. But I'm determined to put those behind me, Daddy. I'm going to make a good life for my baby. We're going to be happy."

Sighing, he patted her cheek and smiled. "I know you will, honey. I just wish...well, I think you'd be a whole lot happier if Cooper made you three a family."

Emily knew that and so did her father. But Cooper was yet to see it and she seriously doubted he ever would.

Forcing a bright smile on her face, Emily patted her father's midsection. "Come on, let's go to the kitchen and I'll make a fresh pot of coffee. Cooper will be back from feeding soon and he'll want a cup, too."

Linking his arm through Emily's, the two of them left

the bedroom and started down the long hallway to the kitchen. As they walked, Harlan said, "Cooper doesn't realize what he has in you."

Emily suddenly stopped in her tracks and turned pleading eyes on her father. "Daddy, please promise me you won't say anything to Cooper about…staying here with me and the baby. Promise?"

He frowned. "I promise. But it wouldn't hurt—"

She shook her head. "Don't you understand? If Cooper ever decides to become a part of our lives, I want him to do it on his own. It has to be that way."

Harlan nodded and Emily sighed with relief. The thought of Cooper leaving tore at her heart. But the idea of forcing him to stay went against every hope, every dream she'd ever had for herself and her baby.

She wasn't going to throw herself at him, nor would she beg him to love her. The only thing she could do now was cherish the short time she had left with him.

# Chapter Nine

More than a week later Emily was cooking supper when Cooper entered the back door with blood oozing down the front of his shirt.

"Cooper!" Tossing the wooden spoon into the bubbling pot of chicken and dumplings, she raced across the room to him. "Oh my Lord, what happened? What have you done?"

He gingerly shrugged the sheepskin coat off his shoulders. Emily caught the garment before it hit the floor and tossed it on a nearby chair.

Turning back to him, she winced at the red stain, which began at his collarbone and ended at the waistband of his jeans.

"It's nothing to get alarmed about," he said calmly. "I jabbed a piece of wire in my shoulder. That's all."

"That's all!" she exclaimed. "Oh, Coop, there's so much blood! Come sit down. Let me see." She grabbed his hand and tugged him over to the table. As soon as he took a seat, she unsnapped his shirt and eased it off his shoulders.

"I'll have to pull my thermal undershirt over my head," he told her.

"No. Don't do that. I'll cut it off." She scurried over to the cabinets and pulled a pair of sewing shears from a drawer. In a matter of seconds she had sliced the thermal material all the way down the front and peeled it back from the wound.

As she bent her head to examine the cut more closely, Cooper's eyes glided over the top of her blond head. This past week, he'd seen a change in Emily. She'd softened and warmed toward him. Every time he turned around she was going out of her way to do something for him. She talked to him constantly and asked his advice on anything and everything. But the change that had struck him the most was the absence of bitterness in her eyes and voice. She no longer looked at him as though she hated him, as though the heartache he caused her in the past was beyond forgiving.

He didn't know why or how the change in her had happened. He had to confess to himself it filled him with joy to see the Emily he'd first fallen in love with. Yet on the other hand, her warmth and open tenderness toward him was making it harder and harder for Cooper to resist her.

"See, I told you it's nothing to be carrying on about," he muttered. His shoulder hurt like hell, but having her this close was even worse. It would be worth bleeding a little longer, he decided, if he could pull her onto his lap and kiss her soft warm mouth.

"It's terrible," she countered. "This needs a few stitches, at least. How did you do it?"

"Stretching barbed wire," he answered. "It broke under pressure and flew back at me."

Emily made a tsking noise as her fingers gently examined the gaping wound just below his collarbone. "I should have been out there helping you. It's a miracle you weren't hit in the face. I knew a man who lost an eye while building a fence.''

"You're hardly in any shape to be working out in the cold now. Besides, I have good reflexes. I jumped back.''

"Apparently not quick enough.'' Straightening to her full height, she made a visual inspection of his face. He might want to brush the injury off as nothing more than a deep scratch, but Emily could see he was pale and in a great deal of pain. Everything in her wanted to comfort him, to touch his face and kiss his lips and assure him she would always take care of him. But he didn't want that from her. All he needed was a little bit of practical nursing.

"Before we eat supper I think we should drive to the hospital emergency room in Ruidoso. You need to be stitched up before you lose any more blood. And you'll need a tetanus shot.''

"Tetanus hell! I've had so many tetanus shots down through the years I could go for the rest of my life and never need one.''

Seeing she had a stubborn patient on her hands, Emily placed her hands on her hips and scowled at him. "It's incredible to me that you big tough men start running scared at the mention of a needle. And I hardly think you're a medical authority on tetanus.''

He shot her a bored look of disbelief. "Look, Emily, if I get lockjaw from this, you can say I told you so and I won't be able to open my mouth back at you. Besides, an old-timer I once knew gave me a cure for it.''

Emily couldn't help but smile at that. "Really? Then maybe you should let me in on it just in case you do come down with the disease.''

"Simple. Just stick the end of a case knife between my teeth and give it a little whack. The vibration will pop my jaws wide open,'' he said.

The twitch of his lips told Emily he was teasing. At least partially and she chuckled at his nonsense. "Okay, so we've got that problem taken care of. What about the gaping hole in your chest?''

''It's not gaping. Get something to clean it out and we'll pull it together with some tape.''

''Oh, well, I should have thought about that,'' she said with a roll of her eyes. ''A piece of tape should fix it right up.''

''Emily,'' he began only to have her shake her head and start out of the kitchen.

''Don't worry, I'm not going to call 911. Just stay where you are. I'm going to go fetch a first-aid kit from the bathroom.''

When she returned a few moments later Cooper hadn't moved except to pull off the bloody thermal undershirt. The sight of him sitting in the kitchen bare chested was a shock to her senses. For years, she'd carried the muscular beauty of his body in her memory. But that image couldn't compare to the actual thing.

Stepping over to the table, she tried to draw in several calming breaths without him noticing. ''If I had any sense at all,'' she told him, ''I would ignore you and call Aunt Justine over here. She could sew this up.''

''You're making too much of a fuss about this.''

Steadying one hand on his shoulder, Emily dabbed a cotton ball soaked in peroxide against the wound. Cooper tried not to wince as pain shot through his shoulder and down his side.

''I've had all sorts of gouges and scrapes before,'' he said through clenched teeth. ''I'll heal.''

His skin was smooth and warm beneath her fingers, enticing her thoughts and her eyes away from the cut. Turning her head ever so slightly, she discovered his face was only inches from hers. She could feel his soft breath on her cheeks, see the dark gray flecks in his eyes and beneath her breast, her heart felt as if it were surely going to stop.

''If you're lucky, you'll heal,'' she murmured huskily.

"The only thing I've ever been lucky at was staying on the back of a bucking horse," he said lowly, his eyes dropping to her lips.

Emily's heart suddenly jolted back to life and she began to shake all the way down to her toes. "Cooper, I'd better—"

"Forget about the hole in my chest," he said roughly. "Come here and kiss me."

The invitation was the last thing she expected from him. A shudder of anticipation rippled through her as she inched her face near his. With a needy groan, Cooper pulled her onto his lap, then cupping her chin in the palm of his hand, he brought his lips down on hers.

Mindful of his wound, Emily curled her arms around his neck and drew herself closer. He tasted so male, so good, and oh so achingly familiar. She wanted to sink into him, bury her hands into his hair, hold him to her forever.

Her whole body was burning with need when Cooper finally lifted his head and gazed down at her face. Through the haze of her desire, Emily could see regret twisting his features.

"Dear Lord, what sort of man am I?" he asked, his voice rough with emotion.

"Cooper, why—"

His hand suddenly splayed across her swollen belly. "My brother's child is growing inside you, but it doesn't seem to make any difference. I still want you. I want to hold you, make love to you. I want it to be as it was before with us. But—"

Reaching up, she placed her hands on either side of his face. "It's what I want, too, Cooper. Can't you see that? Can't you feel it when we kiss?"

His groan was full of anguish. "It's crazy."

"I think it's perfectly normal for two people to want each other," she reasoned.

He closed his eyes against the beauty of her face. "It isn't right."

"Why?"

His hand moved gently against her and the baby and Emily realized that Cooper honestly wanted to love her, he was simply too afraid to try. William and Kenneth had done that to him, she thought sadly. But then so had she by not trusting him, by not having the faith in him that he'd rightly deserved.

"Because…you belonged to Kenneth," he answered.

She shook her head as her forefinger traced a gentle path down his whiskered jaw. "But he's gone. My life with him is over and will never be again."

He opened his eyes and she searched their gray depths.

"Cooper," she went on, "if I could bring Kenneth back, I would. I never wanted him to die. But I can honestly say I wouldn't go back to being his wife. It wouldn't have been right for either of us."

"Emily, don't say such things to me."

Love filled her eyes as she looked at him. "Why? Because you know they're true? Cooper, your father or brother is no longer dictating your life. You can make your own choices now. Until you realize that you're never going to be happy."

He didn't know what she meant by his life being dictated. He only knew he would never be happy without Emily. And as far as he could see he didn't have any choice in the matter.

Gently he eased her off his lap. "You'd better tape me up so we can eat supper."

"If that's the way you want it."

He glanced at her and the yearning on her face was almost more than he could take.

"It's not the way I want it. But it's the way it has to be."

That night Cooper went to bed early. At supper Emily gave him two painkillers for the cut on his shoulder and the pills eased the ache somewhat. Cooper had been telling her the truth when he'd said he'd had plenty of cuts and gashes down through the years and, like her, he'd known the injury had needed stitches. But he'd purposely made little of the wound because he hadn't wanted to alarm her. Nor had he wanted to jostle her for fifteen or twenty minutes over rough roads in order for him to go to the emergency room.

For the past couple of days she'd appeared more tired than usual and he knew the growing weight of the baby was making it difficult for her to remain on her feet for any length of time. A part of him wanted her pregnancy to be over with so her discomfort would end. But the other part knew that time would be here sooner than he wanted.

With a heavy sigh, he rolled onto his good shoulder and glanced at the red numbers illuminated on a nearby alarm clock. Twelve-thirty. He'd been tossing back and forth on the mattress for hours, unable to get Emily and the words she'd said to him, out of his mind.

*Your father and brother aren't here to dictate your life anymore. You can make your own choices now.*

Cooper still couldn't figure why she'd said such a thing to him or what she'd meant by it. He'd always thought he'd been his own man and chosen his own paths. But now she was forcing him to take another look at himself.

"Cooper?"

The sound of her voice shocked him out of his thoughts. He flipped onto his back and saw her shape silhouetted in the open door of his bedroom.

"I'm awake. What is it?" Dear God, if she'd come to his room to ask him to make love to her, he knew he wouldn't be able to resist.

"I don't know, exactly," she said, her voice strained. "I think I'm having labor pains."

Cooper shot straight up in the bed and switched on the bedside lamp. "You think? You don't know?"

She pressed a hand against the tight drawing pain in her side. "Cooper, I've never had a baby before. I only know how it feels to have a miscarriage."

Cooper didn't want to think about her losing the first baby. His baby. Each time the thought passed through his mind, his heart felt as heavy as a stone.

"It isn't time for you to go into labor," he said pointedly. "Maybe it's just a stomachache. You did eat a raw apple before you went to bed."

She took a deep breath, hoping the pain would ease. After a moment it completely disappeared. "I eat apples all the time. They don't give me a stomachache."

As soon as she got the words out, she could feel the same drawing, burning pain building all over again only this time it was much worse.

Since Cooper was wearing a pair of colored boxer shorts, he didn't hesitate to throw back the covers and rise to his feet. "Do you want me to call the doctor?"

"I know I still have six weeks to go. But something is definitely wrong. The pain is getting…" She bent over double as another hard cramp tore through her.

"Where is Dr. Bellamy's number?"

"On the telephone stand in the living room. It's pasted on the bottom of the phone," she told him, once she'd managed to catch her breath. "But I'm not sure…maybe you shouldn't take time to make the call. I think you'd better drive me into the hospital."

His eyes widened on her. "Dear God, Emily, is it that bad?"

She nodded for an answer. He hurried over to her and took her by the elbow. "Let me help you lie down and then I'll go start the truck and get your coat and bag."

With his arm around the back of her waist, they took

one step forward and then she let out a loud gasp. Cooper stared in horror as amniotic fluid soaked the tail of her long gown and puddled on the floor around their feet.

"Emily!"

"Get me to the bed. The baby is coming!"

Cooper reached to sweep her up in his arms, but she quickly shook her head. "Cooper, don't pick me up. It will tear open the cut on your shoulder."

He couldn't believe she was thinking about him at a time like this.

"Forget the damn cut," he growled and quickly lifted her in his arms and carried her over to his bed. After he'd settled her head on the pillow and covered her with the sheet, he said, "I'm going to call for an ambulance."

"Ambulance? Cooper, the ground is covered with snow. It's like a blizzard out there. Your truck could probably make it—" Her words halted as another pain struck her. Afterward, she heaved out a heavy breath. "We'd do just as well to go in your truck."

Cooper hadn't looked outside since suppertime. He wasn't aware it had started to snow. A damn blizzard is the last thing they needed to happen now!

"There's not enough room for you to lie down in the truck," he reasoned as his mind raced with the slim choices presented to them.

Emily gripped his forearm, fearful to let him leave her even for a minute. "Forget about the ambulance, they'll never make it out here in time," she pleaded through clenched jaws.

Seeing the sheer terror in her eyes, Cooper decided the best thing he could do at this moment was to calm her down and reassure her that everything was going to be all right. He couldn't let her see he was probably more frightened than she was. Dear God, he'd helped cows calve and mares foal but he knew nothing about birthing a baby.

Easing down on the edge of the mattress, he unwrapped her fingers from around his forearm and pressed them between both his hands. "Emily, darling, don't be frightened. You're a healthy woman. You're going to get through this fine. God knows, I won't let anything happen to you."

Most likely William Dunn had said the same thing to Cooper's mother. But he couldn't let himself think about Laura Dunn dying while he was being born. He had to put it out of his mind and be strong and steady for Emily and the baby.

"You're right," she said, her lips trembling with a weak smile. "Having a baby is a natural thing for a woman. I can do it."

Returning her smile, he touched his fingertips against her cheek. "You can do anything."

Her blue gaze clung to his. "As long as you help me."

Emotion swelled in his chest. He tried to push it away and remember his time with her would all be over soon.

"I'll do all I can," he murmured, then quickly left for the living room and the telephone.

Less than three minutes later, he returned to Emily's side. A pale blue nightgown was clutched in one hand. "I thought you might want to change out of that wet thing you have on."

She nodded, then reared up off the pillow as pain suddenly surged through the lower part of her body. "Did..." After the one word, she panted for several seconds then tried again, "Did you call for emergency help?"

"Yes. Your uncle Roy is going to take care of everything. Including calling your parents." He didn't go on to tell her that her suspicions were right. The weather conditions had turned into an all-out blizzard, forcing traffic off the road or, at best, a crawl. Even worse, most of the emergency transport units had been called to a vehicle pileup in the mountains.

"He said to tell you not to worry, Justine says first babies take several hours of labor before they make an appearance into the world. You'll be in the hospital long before then."

Emily looked anything but reassured. "I hope she's right. But the way these pains are coming I don't think I'll be that lucky."

She tugged the dirty gown she was wearing up over her hip, then held up her arms so that Cooper could pull the garment the rest of the way over her head.

Glancing away from him, she murmured, "I'm sorry you have to see me this way."

He picked up the clean gown and searched for the neck. "Emily, don't be embarrassed. I've seen you before."

"Yes. But I was slim then. Not like this."

She was having labor pains and not one medically trained person was around to help her. That it should matter how she looked to him now, amazed Cooper.

"You've always been beautiful to me, Emily. Even now." And he couldn't have meant it more.

He slipped the ring of fabric over her head. She glanced up at him and her eyes told him how grateful she was for his words, his touch, for simply being at her side.

"Just wait a few more minutes and you'll change your mind about that," she tried to joke.

He helped her get the gown down as far as the top of her hips, then covered her with the sheet.

"Now what?" he asked, feeling as helpless as a calf stranded on the wrong side of the fence.

Emily shook her head. "I don't—"

Unable to finish because of another racking pain, Cooper glanced at his watch. From what he'd seen on TV it was important to time the pains and see how frequently they were coming.

Once Emily was able to talk again, she reached for his hand and squeezed it. "Cooper, do you think something is wrong with the baby? Answer me truthfully. If you think it's a possibility, tell me.''

Concern marring his features, he eased back onto the side of the bed. ''Was the baby moving earlier this evening?''

Nodding, she bit down on her lip and tried not to cry. ''Nothing seemed out of the ordinary. When I visited Dr. Bellamy at the first of the week, he said the baby's heart sounded good and its head was down in the birthing position. But that sometimes happens weeks before.''

He pushed strands of blond hair off her face. ''Then what makes you think something might be wrong?''

Her worried gaze clung to his. ''Because it's too early. Usually premature births happen when something is wrong.''

''Emily, honey, you're borrowing trouble. I'll bet that little fella of yours just decided he couldn't wait any longer to see what was going on out here. Besides, the doctor's calculation on the due date could be wrong.''

That was true enough, Emily thought. Her cycle had never been regular so Dr. Bellamy had more or less guessed as best he could on the due date. She tried to relax, but another pain was building in her back, tearing through her sides like a hot branding iron. By the time it was over she felt utterly drained.

''I think you should go get some clean towels from the bathroom,'' she said weakly.

He tried his best to appear calm, even though another glance at his watch told him it had been less than a minute since Emily's last pain.

''I'll be right back,'' he assured her.

For the next fifteen minutes Emily's pain continued to increase in severity. Cooper used a cool cloth to wipe the sweat from her face, but other than that he could do little else for her.

Though he kept it carefully hidden, he was inwardly

cursing the weather, the untimeliness of her labor and most of all the fact he couldn't make it all better for her. Each time the pain tore through her, he wanted to ram his fist through a wall. Instead, he gripped her hands and murmured anything he could think of to encourage her.

"I'm going to go look out the front," he told her. "I might be able to see some lights coming."

She shook her head. "Cooper, I'm in labor, I'm not crazy. It will take an ambulance forever to get here."

"Well, your dad or uncle Roy might make it sooner in one of their four-wheel-drive vehicles."

"I wouldn't get in it now—"

Cooper felt as if his own insides were tearing as he watched the agony twist her face.

"Emily? Are you all right?" He'd asked her that question many times already, but he supposed he needed reassuring as much as she did.

Her knees were already drawn up. She motioned for him to pull back the sheet. "I—think the baby is coming! Now!"

He couldn't be shaken by the sight of her blood. Nor could he let himself think for one moment how his own mother had taken her last breath after giving birth to him. It wasn't going to be that way for Emily. She was more precious than his own life to him. He had to do everything in his power to get her through this. Her and the baby!

Pulling back the sheet, he pushed the tail of her gown out of the way and bent down for a closer look. "I can— yes, I think I can see the crown of his head!"

"Oh, thank God," she said weakly, then strained up off the pillow as another tremendous pain consumed her.

"Emily, I think—all you need to do now is bear down and push."

"I'm trying—I don't have much strength—left," she groaned, then gasped in several long breaths.

He grabbed the washcloth from the nightstand and wiped her hot brow. "I know, darling, I know. But try. It'll soon be over and the pain will stop."

With everything inside her, Emily bore down again. And again. Cooper clasped the inner part of her thighs and willed the little head forward.

"That's it, Emily! It's coming! Once more and the baby will be here!"

Her head swimming with pain and exhaustion, she tried to do as he instructed. Then suddenly Cooper was shouting excitedly and she felt the blessed relief of the baby passing out of her.

Cooper quickly grabbed the newborn and turned him facedown so any mucus would drain out of his mouth rather than in.

"He's a boy, Emily!"

"But is he breathing? Is he all right?"

As Cooper massaged the tiny back, a loud squal emitted from the baby. He sagged with joy and relief.

"He's breathing all right. Listen to that voice!"

With a clean towel, he wiped as much of the afterbirth from the baby as he could, then lay it on Emily's stomach. "I figure he'll be much happier there than anywhere else. Besides, I'm not sure about cutting the umbilical cord. I'll let the doctor do that."

Tears of joy streamed down Emily's face as she brought her hand up to the baby's red, wrinkled cheek. Her child was here and safe.

"Oh, Coop, thank you," she whispered weakly. "Thank you for bringing my baby into the world."

Cooper's eyes brimmed with tears, but he managed to blink them away before Emily could see them.

"I didn't do anything, Emily. You did it all."

He eased down beside mother and child, who was still

bawling as though he wanted everyone in Lincoln county to know he'd arrived.

Rubbing a finger over the infant's damp head, Cooper looked to Emily's drained but joyous face. "He's beautiful. Like his mother."

Her hand crept to Cooper's arm and she tugged weakly. He leaned closer as emotion balled in his throat.

She kissed his cheek, then smiled up at him. "You're my hero, Coop. You always have been."

## Chapter Ten

"Emily, he's absolutely perfect. He couldn't have looked more like you if he'd been stamped from a mold."

Emily smiled at her mother who had just returned from her third trip from the hospital nursery.

"You sound like a typical grandmother."

Laughing, Rose took a seat in the vinyl chair beside her daughter's bed. "Of course I do. It's my right."

Emily scooted to a sitting position and pushed her tumbled hair away from her face. Nearly twelve hours had passed since an ambulance had arrived at the ranch and took her and the baby to the hospital. Cooper had rode in with them. But he'd had Harlan take him back home earlier this morning to take care of feeding the cattle and horses.

Since then, Emily had recuperated nicely. Other than being sore and a little weak, she'd managed so far to shower and eat a big lunch. As for the baby, he'd already nursed at her breast and Emily was still in a euphoric daze at being a mother.

Rose made a motion with her hand around the room. "Judging from all the flowers and balloons in here, everybody is as happy as I am about the baby. It looks like a florist shop in here.''

Emily pointed to a potted calla lilly a nurse's aide had brought in a few minutes earlier and placed on the bedside table. ''Another one came while you were down at the nursery. It's from Charlie.''

Rose leaned up in her seat and pulled the card nestled amongst the lush green leaves. ''Way to go, Em! Hope I can see you and the new baby soon. Love, Charlie,'' Rose read, then smiled winsomely. ''You and Charlie became buddies the first time you saw each other.''

Emily chuckled. ''I had just become a teenager and Charlie was six. He wore a holstered cap pistol on his hips and pretended he was the Durango Kid. Now he's all grown up, handsome, and a bona fide Texas Ranger. I can only hope my son turns out as well as Charlie.''

''Charlie is a wonderful guy,'' Rose agreed. ''But I don't want my grandson to be a lawman. I'd worry about him all the time, just like Justine does Charlie.''

Emily didn't necessarily want her son to be a lawman, either. But she would never tell him he couldn't be. She wanted him to grow up to be his own man, strong and self-assured.

''Right now I'm just relieved my son is healthy. Since he weighed seven pounds and was fully developed right down to his fingernails, Dr. Bellamy says he was conceived much sooner than he'd first calculated.''

''And I just thank God you and Cooper had the good sense to know what to do. Your daddy and I are both relieved.''

At the mention of Cooper's name, Emily let out a wistful sigh. ''Oh, Mother, you can't imagine how wonderful Cooper was through it all. I'm beginning to think he might really...care for me and the baby.''

Rose smiled gently at her daughter's glowing face. ''I've always thought so.''

Emily glanced down at the thermal blanket covering her lap. "I've been praying that he's changed his mind about leaving. Especially now that he's seen the baby. But I—"

A knock on the door cut her sentence short. Rose went over to invite the caller in. When she saw it was Cooper, she quickly informed her daughter she was going to the cafeteria for a little lunch.

"I didn't mean to run your mother off," he said, as he stepped inside the room. It was filled with all sorts of potted plants and cut flowers. Bright balloons with words of congratulations were tied to the foot of the bed and the handles of several cups of candy sat on the windowsill. Feeling like an idiot for only having a hat in his hands, he moved toward her and the bed.

Emily's heart soared at the sight of him. He was dressed in dark jeans and a rust colored shirt. His face was clean shaven and his hair brushed into neat waves. He'd always looked good to her under any conditions, but now after all they'd been through together, it was like falling in love with him all over again and her joy shone like a light on her face.

"You didn't make Mother leave," she assured him. "She's been here all morning. It's time she got out of here and went to lunch."

Smiling at him, she motioned for him to take the seat her mother had just vacated. "Have you had your lunch? Did you remember there was a bowl of chicken and dumplings left over in the fridge?"

He hadn't thought about eating, much less what was in the refrigerator. "I ate a little snack. Don't worry about me. What about yourself?"

She patted her stomach, which felt absurdly flat to her now. "I stuffed myself at lunch. The baby did, too. Did you go down to the nursery and look at him?"

Cooper hadn't planned on it, but the minute he'd stepped into the hospital corridor something had come over him.

He'd went straight to the nursery and stared through the window for long minutes at Emily's new son.

"He looks like you."

Emily chuckled softly. "That's what Mother and Daddy and the rest of my family say. They also think you're wonderful for delivering him."

A ruddy flush crossed his cheeks. "I didn't do anything. I just happened to be there."

She shot him an engaging smile. "Now, Coop, there's no need for you to be humble about it."

Emily was like an excited kid at Christmas, Cooper thought, and she was trying to include him in her joy. Oh God, she was making this even harder on him.

Propping his ankle on his knee, he stared at the toe of his brown boot. "Have you decided what to name him yet?"

"I have. If you agree."

Surprise arching his brows, he glanced at her. "Me? What do I have to do with it?"

Her smile quavered. "Well, you might not like what I have in mind. If you don't, be honest and tell me."

"Emily, you shouldn't be worrying about my opinion. I wouldn't know the first thing about naming a baby, anyway."

Her eyes continued to hold his and her heart thumped with love. "Well, you might in this case. I want to name him Harlan Cooper Dunn. After my father and you. If that's all right with you."

Cooper was stunned. He'd never expected her to name her child after him. He didn't know what to think or say.

"Emily—are you sure?"

She leaned over and reached for his hand. He gave it to her because he had to, because at that moment he needed to touch her just one more time.

"Of course I'm sure. I think it's a strong, wonderful name that my baby can be proud of." She desperately wanted to say *our* baby, but she still wasn't sure how he was feeling. Last night she'd been certain he looked at her with love, touched her with love. But now, today, he seemed different and her heart began to pound with dread. "I only hope that he grows to live up to his name."

"If that's the way you really feel, then I'd be honored."

She let out a breath of relief. All this time she'd felt as if Cooper resented the baby. But after seeing the gentle way he handled her son last night, she couldn't believe he didn't have a bit of tenderness in his heart.

"Thank you, Cooper. I'm so glad you approve." She squeezed his hand and a smile returned to her face. "Was everything all right at the ranch? Did you give Native Moon an extra block of alfalfa?"

He'd even given Emily's Appaloosa a brushing, but he wasn't going to tell her. He didn't want her thinking he'd grown soft and sentimental. Once he was gone, she needed to think he'd been happy to go. It would be easier that way.

"Yes. I did."

"Oh, thank you. And, Cooper, before you head back to the ranch, would you mind picking up a few baby bottles at the store? I know I'm breast-feeding, but he'll need some water now and then. Aunt Justine and Chloe have a date set next month for a baby shower." She laughed and gave his hand another squeeze. "But since little Harlan Cooper decided to make an early appearance, I don't have anything I need yet."

"When are you and the baby going home?"

She grimaced. "In the morning. As far as I'm concerned I'm ready to go now." She glanced away from him suddenly and Cooper wondered at the faint blush on her cheeks. "I'm sorry I made such a mess of your bed. But now—" Pausing, she looked back at him. "I'm glad the baby was born in your bed. It seems right somehow."

He closed his eyes at the memory of her writhing in pain, calling his name and gripping his hands so tightly at times his fingers had gone numb. He'd hated seeing her in so much agony and hated even more that he hadn't been able to do anything about it. For as long as he lived, Cooper knew he would never forget last night or the fear and joy that had swept through him as Emily's baby had slipped into the world.

"I'm glad it's all over for you."

Smiling, she patted her flat stomach. "In a few weeks, I'll be able to ride Native Moon all the way to the back of the ranch." Her glance at him was suggestive. "That is, if I can talk you into doing a little baby-sitting. But don't worry," she added before he could make any sort of response. "I won't make a habit of it. Just now and then when I get the urge to ride."

She was killing him with her words and smile and touch. He had to open his mouth and tell her why he was really here before he lost his courage.

"Uh...Emily, I think—" With her hand still holding onto his, he moved from the chair to the side of her bed.

"Yes?" she asked, her eyes glowing at having him even closer.

He drew in a bracing breath and tried to look away, but something about her beautiful face wouldn't let him. "When I leave the hospital I won't be going back to the ranch."

Her brows lifted. "Oh, you have some other chores to do? If that's the case, then don't bother about the baby bottles. I'll have Mother pick them up before we leave the hospital in the morning. I know you have more than you can do as it is. And I've been thinking a lot about that, Cooper."

Distracted by her words, he looked at her curiously. "You've been thinking about what?"

"About hiring another man to help you on the ranch. I know we don't necessarily have the money to pay anyone wages, but we would—if I went back to work."

Cooper was astounded. "Back to work? Emily, you have a baby now. For Pete's sake this isn't the time to be taking on a job!"

She quickly shook her head. "Not an outside job. But for this first year of little Harlan Cooper's life I'm going to be pretty much tied to the house. I can easily do accounts for people while I watch the baby. It would give us the extra money to hire a wrangler and then you wouldn't have to work so hard."

That she was willing to do such a thing was incredible to Cooper. Especially when he knew how long she'd hoped and dreamed of having a child. Now her dream had finally come true, yet she was willing to sacrifice a part of her time to make life better for him. Oh God, he had to get out of here before he crumbled, before he began to think it was his right to stay and make a family with her and the baby.

"Emily, it's kind of you to offer, but I believe you'll be plenty busy taking care of your son. Besides…I'm not…going to be on the ranch anymore. After today."

Cooper might as well have slapped her. She stared at him in stunned silence for so long that he was finally forced to look away and swallow at the bitter lump in his throat.

"Oh," she said quietly.

He gave her one stiff nod of his head. "I've already hired a man to take care of the ranch. In fact, he's already there now. Your father had suggested him for the job before, so I know he'll be trustworthy. And he's likable, too. He and his family live in Hondo, so he'll be driving back and forth every day to the Diamond D."

Emily's gaze dropped to the blanket covering her bed. Since the first night she'd found Cooper in the barn, she'd known he would be leaving. She'd told herself over and over to get prepared to say goodbye to him. Because Cooper Dunn wasn't a staying sort of man. But her heart hadn't listened to logic. The longer he'd stayed, the more she'd wanted to believe it would be forever. What a fool she'd been!

"I see. So...uh—" She forced herself to look up at him and smile as though nothing was wrong while inside she was really dying. "I guess you're going back to rodeo?"

Cooper wasn't going back to rodeo. He'd had enough of that fast, rough and tumble life. But he wasn't going to tell Emily his decision just now. He figured it would be best to let her think he was leaving to get back to his career, not to get away from her.

"Well, San Antonio is coming up this next week and it's one of the biggest rodeos of the year."

The pain in her chest was so terrible she could hardly breathe. "You certainly wouldn't want to miss it. I guess it's a good thing little Harlan decided to make an early appearance."

"Oh, Emily—"

There was a slight break in his voice and as she studied his dark face it dawned on her that his leaving was hurting him almost as much as it was her.

"Don't feel badly, Cooper. You've told me all along you'd be leaving after the baby arrived. I didn't realize you meant so soon afterward, but that's okay. I'll be fine. We'll both be fine."

He tried his best to appear cheerful, but he'd never been much of an actor and the way he felt it would have taken an Academy Award performance to hide his misery.

"Of course you'll be fine," he told her. "And I'll be calling from time to time and sending money."

Emily didn't want his money. Nor would she use it for herself or the baby. But she wasn't going to argue the issue with him now. She didn't want to waste these last precious moments. Later, she'd put the money in a savings account and figure out what to do with it. But first she had to figure out how to stop this tearing pain in her heart.

"I...hope you'll be careful. I'm not keen on the idea of

your climbing on those rank horses. But…I know it's your job and you love it.''

He didn't love riding broncs. He loved her. But his feelings didn't matter. They couldn't matter.

"Don't worry about me, Emily. I'm like a cat, I always land on my feet.''

Emily wanted to grab his arm and tug him down to her. She wanted to grip the back of his neck, whisper in his ear how much she needed him. How much she loved him. But she'd hardly kept her feelings a secret from him. She'd told him in a thousand ways what he meant to her. To go into it again now would only make things unbearably awkward for the both of them.

"I hope you're right." She forced her eyes up at him, but his gaze was on the windows and the falling snow. "Are you already packed and ready to go?''

He nodded, then looked down at her. "Yeah. And the weather back toward Texas is clearing, so I'll probably be out of the snow by this afternoon.''

He was heading to San Antonio. But where then? she wondered. Other than the Diamond D, he had no home to go to when he was tired and lonely. His life would consist of the road, motels and bucking chutes. He wanted those things more than her and the baby. The whole idea was crushing her.

"Will you go down to the nursery and look at Harlan Cooper before you leave?''

The thought of saying goodbye to the little fella again tore at Cooper's heart, but he could see how important it was to her. He'd let her down so many times and his leaving now was probably the biggest disappointment he'd ever given her. Seeing the baby one last time was the least he could do for her.

"Yes. I will.''

She tried to smile but her lips were trembling so badly she barely managed a faint grin.

Cooper couldn't stand another minute. He leaned down and pressed a brief kiss on her cheek, then headed toward the door. Yet the call of his name stopped him and he was forced to look back at her one more time.

"I just want you to remember the Diamond D will always be your home," she said lowly. "If you ever feel the need to come back…it will be waiting for you. And so will I."

Even with the snowplows out working, the highways were treacherous leading away from Ruidoso. For the past thirty minutes Cooper had been forced to little more than a crawl, but he'd hardly noticed he'd only managed to travel ten miles.

Whether he was going fast or slow, the result was still the same. He was leaving Emily. Again. Was he crazy? Was there something lacking in him? Why couldn't he sink down roots and say Emily was *his* woman and Harlan Cooper was *his* son?

Everything inside of Cooper was screaming for him to turn around and go back to her. But each time the notion to put his boot on the brakes came into his head, another part of him hollered whoa.

He wasn't a family man. He didn't know anything about it. And Emily had already been put through enough hell by the Dunn men. If she knew what was good for her, she'd never want to see him again.

With him out of the way, he reasoned with himself, she could find herself a strong man, one that would be a good father to her son. Hell, Cooper didn't know anything about being a daddy. He'd barely had one himself. Little Harlan deserved better. Much better. He wanted the boy to know how much he was loved and that the Diamond D would always be his home for as long as he wanted.

But would the next man Emily found do all that for the

boy? Would the next man even give a damn about the ranch?

Groaning inwardly, Cooper gripped the steering wheel even tighter. Dear God, he didn't want to think of Emily with some other man. She was meant to be his. The baby was meant to be his.

*Your brother and your father are gone now. You're a grown man, free to make your own choices.*

Pulling to the side of the road, he stared out at the distant, snow capped mountains. This high desert country was where he'd grown up and where he'd called home. He'd left it because he'd had no choice. His brother had virtually shut him out of the ranch. Though he hadn't been able to see it then, he could now. He'd been slowly exorcised of his home and the woman he loved. Maybe Cooper had let it happen. Or maybe he hadn't realized just what a manipulator Kenneth had been.

Whatever the case, Cooper had been blessed with another chance to claim what was justly his. He had a choice this time. And this time the choice he made had to be right.

When Rose returned to her daughter's room after lunch, she found Emily in the bathroom trying to wash tearstains from her face.

"Emily! What's wrong? Are you in pain? I'll call Dr. Bellamy."

The older woman quickly turned to leave the room. Emily managed to catch her by the shoulder.

"No. Don't bother the doctor. I'm all right."

Frowning with disbelief, Rose took her by the arm and led her slowly back over to the bed.

Once Emily was sitting on the side of the mattress, Rose said, "You're not all right. You look awful."

Emily sniffed and reached for a tissue on the bedside table. "I know I do. I shouldn't have cried. But I…couldn't help it."

Her voice broke on the last few words and she began to sob all over again. Rose made a tsking noise with her tongue.

"I want you to answer me two things. Do you need medical attention?"

"No."

"Is the baby okay?"

"Yes. As far as I know, he's fine."

Rose breathed with relief. "Then why all this crying as if the world is ending? Are you feeling lost because you can't feel the baby moving inside you anymore? I know that happens to a lot of women after they give birth. It happened to me after your brother Ethan was born."

Emily shook her head. If only it were that simple, she thought miserably. "No. It's not that. It's…Cooper. He's left."

Rose chuckled softly. "Well, darling, you can't expect him to sit around a hospital room with you all day. Men like him and your daddy just aren't equipped for it. I'm sure he had lots to do back at the ranch."

"Oh, Mother!" she wailed. "I mean he's left Lincoln County. And he's not coming back. At least probably not for a long time."

As Rose digested this news, she quietly regarded her daughter's face. "And why did he leave? Did he tell you?"

Emily shrugged. "Ever since he first came back, he told me he'd be leaving eventually. He says he can't be a husband and father. He's gone back to rodeo. Damn it!" She blew her nose, then sniffed again. "Those horses are going to kill him! He's going to wind up just like his brother."

Rose shook her head with solemn conviction. "No. Cooper will never be like Kenneth. Thank God."

Emily's bent head lifted and she studied her mother for long moments. "Why do you say it like that?"

"Because the two men were never anything alike."

"That's true," Emily mumbled after a moment. "Kenneth never wanted to leave the Diamond D and Cooper never wanted to stay on it.''

Rose said thoughtfully, "Perhaps Cooper had to leave for financial reasons, Emily. After all, none of us are made of money and Cooper has sunk several thousand into the ranch these past few months without getting anything in return. He probably needs a paycheck or two and was too full of pride to admit it to you.''

Emily groaned. Her mother was always so sensible and practical. And Emily had always tried very hard to follow her example. Rose had always been a beautiful goddess of a woman plus she was blessed with common sense and gentle ways. But this was one time Rose's optimistic belief in people was pure bull.

"Mother, Cooper didn't leave because he was in need of money. He left because little Harlan finally got here and he could go on his way without worrying about me being pregnant and alone on the ranch.''

Rose smiled and then her smile turned into soft laughter. "Oh, daughter dear, you sound so silly. Do you hear what you're saying?''

"Yes!'' she exclaimed as a spurt of anger shot through her. "Cooper shot out of here like a cat with a scalded tail. He couldn't wait to leave us!''

"Could be he thought you wanted him to go.''

Staring with disbelief at her mother, she exclaimed, "He knew better! I asked him to stay.''

"You said those very words to him today? You said, Cooper, I love you and I want you to stay on the ranch with me and the baby?''

Emily's cheeks flamed scarlet. "Well, not exactly like that. I mean, I didn't ask him to stay today. I could see he'd already made up his mind to go. What was I supposed to do, beg?''

Rose's expression turned admonishing. "I hope you did remind him how you feel about him.'' When Emily failed to respond, Rose grasped her daughter by the shoulder. "Emily, you did tell him you loved him?"

Emily gave her one miserable shake of her head. "No. Do you think it would have made a difference?"

Rose nodded gravely. "Sometimes it makes all the difference in the world. It did when your daddy said it to me."

Emily jumped up from the bedside, but immediately groped for a handhold as dizziness turned the room into a whirling kaleidoscope.

Rose quickly grabbed her daughter by the arm. "Emily, are you deliberately trying to hurt yourself? You can't be moving around that quickly. Before you realize what's happened you'll be on the floor in a dead faint."

"I...have to go after him, Mother. I have to tell him, *really* tell him how I feel."

"Darling, you've just had a baby! You can't go running off anywhere."

"Then you have to send Daddy after him. Please, Mother! Go call him and tell him. Maybe he can intercept him on highway 70 before he gets to Roswell. Cooper is going to San Antonio. That's the route he'll probably take."

Rose pressed her daughter back onto the bed. "Okay, I'll go call your daddy. But you first have to promise to calm down."

Emily breathed in deeply and nodded. "I will. I know I'm acting a bit hysterical, but, Mother...I love the man so. I don't want to live for ten more years without him!"

Rose patted her daughter's cheek. "You won't have to. My father was a gambling man. And if I were like him, right now I'd bet the Bar M that Cooper will be back soon. Probably before the night is over."

Emily wearily closed her eyes. "Then you'd lose the family ranch."

Rose was about to reply when she was interrupted by a knock on the door. She crossed the small room to open it, then seeing who was standing on the other side, she turned and gave her daughter a broad smile.

"No. I haven't lost the family ranch. I think I've just gained a son-in-law."

With the caller still partially hidden behind the door, Emily frowned irritably at her mother. "What are you talking about?"

She waved a dismissive hand at Emily. "I'm going down to the cafeteria for pie and coffee."

"You just had lunch! Are you..." Rose disappeared around the door, then Emily's jaws suddenly went slack and her heart began to chug with the speed of a runaway locomotive.

"Cooper," she breathed.

Without a word he walked to her bed and it was then she realized he was holding more than just his hat in his hands. He handed her a single red rose, its long stem wrapped in cellophane.

As she looked at the perfectly formed petals, her throat filled with such a ball of emotion she couldn't speak.

"I know the rose is a little late in coming," he said gently. "A whole lot late. But I hope it will still mean something to you."

She looked up at him and her eyes welled with tears. "I don't understand, Coop. What does it mean? Why are you here?"

He sat down beside her and she was suddenly so overwhelmed with his closeness and the look of longing on his face that tears fell from her eyes and she dropped her forehead against his chest.

"Oh, darling! Emily, don't cry," he whispered as his hand made gentle circles on her back. "I didn't come back to make you cry."

Emily tilted her head up at him. "Why did you come back?"

"Because it's where I belong."

The unexpectedness of his words dried her tears. "What about your rodeo life? Don't you want to get back to it?"

Cooper shook his head, then circling his arms around her, he pulled her close against him.

"I haven't needed the sport for a long time now. I only kept doing it because it was all I had."

Her wet eyes searched his and suddenly she could see what a lonely life he'd lived these past years he'd been away. She wanted desperately to make up for all he'd lost, to fill his days and nights with love. "I'm so glad you came back, Cooper."

With his thumb and forefinger holding her chin, his gaze continued to probe her face. "Are you really, Emily? I've been so…blind and crazy. How can you trust me now? I left you once before and today—"

Shaking her head, she placed her fingertips against his lips. "Cooper, it's time you realized how much I love you. I regret all those years we missed being together, but I want you to know I'll never blame you for them. I'll never throw them in your face. Please believe that, Coop."

Doubt filled his gray eyes. "When I first came back you hated me."

"I don't know that I hated you. I don't know that I could hate anyone. I like to think I'm like my mother, Rose. She doesn't have the capability to hate anyone. But when you first came back I hurt every time I looked at you. All those years I'd believed you had deserted me. That you had just used me for your own amusement."

Cooper groaned as he imagined how hurt and betrayed she must have felt. "And when did you finally decide it hadn't really been that way?"

"Little by little I began to think I might have been wrong. But until Daddy opened my eyes I don't think I fully realized exactly what had happened back then."

Curious now, he straightened her away from him but still

held firmly to her shoulders. "Your father? He talked to you about us?"

She nodded. "My father and I talk about everything. And he's never guided me wrong. He said that…" Clutching the rose in one hand, she reached for his hand with her free one. "You won't get angry if I tell you?"

He chuckled and Emily's heart soared at the wonderful sound.

"How could I get angry? You told me you loved me. That makes everything bearable."

Oh, Mother, you're wonderful, Emily thought. To Cooper she said, "Daddy believed Kenneth was a manipulator. He said from the time you two boys were very young, your brother worked you and your father against each other. So by the time you had grown into a man, the resentment was already in place. You believed your father hated you and adored Kenneth."

"Well, William Dunn did have a reason for hating me. My being born caused my mother to die. At least he thought so."

"You can't really believe that, Coop. Your mother died from negligence and circumstance."

Cooper looked down at Emily's fingers wrapped tightly around his. It amazed him how much strength he could draw from such a tiny hand.

"You know Emily, for all these years I tried to tell myself you were the one who initiated your marriage to Kenneth. I didn't want to believe my own brother betrayed me in such an underhanded, backstabbing way. It took coming home to open my eyes. But I guess it took driving away this afternoon to really make me take a look at things. Kenneth wanted to get me out of the way—first because he wanted the ranch for himself and second because he wanted you. All that bragging he was doing about my riding skills was probably sticking in his craw. But I fell for it," he said with a self-deprecating snort.

"Only because you'd been made to feel unworthy. You were shut out from the ranch. You had nothing else but your riding." Shaking her head regretfully, she added, "Don't forget, I fell for his lies, too. And I spent ten years living a mistake."

Cupping his hands around her face, he brought his lips against her forehead. At that moment Emily was sure she'd never been given a sweeter kiss.

"I guess we both made mistakes," he said. "But we shouldn't have to go on paying for them."

"We're not going to, Coop. I understand you've had your doubts about putting the past behind us. But we can. The three of us can be a real family...if you want us."

His fingertips traced a gentle pattern across her cheeks. "I want it more than anything. But, Emily, just wanting a family isn't going to make me husband or father material. It scares the hell out of me to think of disappointing you or baby Harlan. There's going to be times I'll probably say and do all the wrong things and I—"

She pressed her cheek against his as joy surged through her like the golden rays of a rainbow. "You'll learn as you go," she whispered, "just like I'm going to learn to be a wife to you and a mother to our son."

He pulled his head back to look at her. "Our son?"

She nodded. "You do want Harlan Cooper to be your son, don't you?"

"Oh, Emily, I...while you were pregnant all I could think was that you were carrying Kenneth's child when it should have been mine. The baby you lost, my baby— whatever you thought then, I would have wanted it. And last night when I held Harlan Cooper for the first moments after he was born, it was like some sort of phenomenon came over me. It no longer mattered whose blood flowed in his veins. He felt like *mine*. I wanted him to be *mine*. Can you believe me?"

Certain her heart was going to burst with happiness,

Emily flung her arms around his neck. "He is yours, darling. You'll always be his one and only father. And more than anything, I want to give you another child—to make up for the one we lost so long ago. Would you like that?"

Humbled by the sheer wonder of her love, he could hardly speak. "You would go through that much pain again to have our child?"

She smiled at him as only a woman could smile at the man she loved and wanted. "I would go through it again. And again. For you, Coop. Don't ever doubt my love."

Cooper didn't know why God had blessed him so or why He had allowed his life to come full circle. But he was certain of one thing, he would never take the happiness he'd been given for granted.

"So when do you think you're going to feel recuperated enough to marry me?"

"Now. Today," she answered quickly, then giggled at the shocked expression on his face. "What's the matter? Getting cold feet already?"

He tugged her closer and placed a long heated kiss on her lips, leaving Emily in no doubt as to what lay in store for her.

"We don't want to get married in a hospital room," he murmured once the kiss had ended. "We want to get married on the Diamond D with lots of flowers and food and your family all around us."

She'd never expected anything so sweet and sentimental from him. Apparently she still had a lot to learn about Cooper Dunn and she was going to love every minute of it.

"Next week is Valentine's Day. It would be the perfect date for a wedding. What do you think?" she asked, the corners of her lips tilting provocatively up at him.

"I think I'll start counting the minutes," he said, his voice growing husky as once again his face dipped toward hers.

A brief knock on the door interrupted Cooper's intentions to seal their wedding date with a kiss. Instead both of them turned their heads to see a nurse and the baby swaddled in a blue receiving blanket entering the room.

The young woman smiled cheerfully at Emily and Cooper. "Which parent wants to hold this little guy first?"

The question had Cooper glancing expectantly at Emily, who in turn pointed a finger back at him.

"Daddy does," Emily told her.

The nurse placed the baby boy in the crook of his arm and as Emily watched him cradle their son against his broad chest, she knew Cooper had really and truly come home to stay.

\*     \*     \*     \*     \*

*And the Murdocks live on! Look for Charlie's story in the fall of 1998, when the Texas Ranger gets caught by a single mom!*

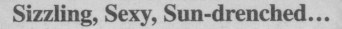

# Take 4 bestselling love stories FREE

## a FREE surprise gift!

## Special Limited-time Offer

**Mail to Silhouette Reader Service™**

3010 Walden Avenue
P.O. Box 1867
Buffalo, N.Y. 14240-1867

**YES!** Please send me 4 free Silhouette Romance™ novels and my free surprise gift. Then send me 6 brand-new novels every month, which I will receive months before they appear in bookstores. Bill me at the low price of $2.90 each plus 25¢ delivery and applicable sales tax, if any* That's the complete price and a savings of over 10% off the cover prices—quite a bargain! I understand that accepting the books and gift places me under no obligation ever to buy any books. I can always return a shipment and cancel at any time. Even if I never buy another book from Silhouette, the 4 free books and the surprise gift are mine to keep forever.

215 SEN CF2P

| Name | (PLEASE PRINT) | |
|------|------|------|
| Address | Apt. No. | |
| City | State | Zip |

This offer is limited to one order per household and not valid to present Silhouette Romance™ subscribers. *Terms and prices are subject to change without notice. Sales tax applicable in N.Y.

USROM-696

©1990 Harlequin Enterprises Limited

**Under the big sky, three unsuspecting couples are granted their**

# BEST-KEPT WISHES

In this heartwarming new miniseries by Carol Grace, three high school friends reveal their dreams on one starry night. Now they're all grown up and about to discover their dearest wishes can come true—with the help of love....

**GRANTED: BIG SKY GROOM**  (#1277, February 1998)
Tally James longed for a ranch of her own—and wealthy rancher Jed Whitmore owned the spread of her dreams. But would a marriage of convenience to the groom who could fulfill all her wishes bring her heartache—or love?

**GRANTED: WILD WEST BRIDE**  (#1303, June 1998)
Rugged Josh Gentry had just about given up on happily-ever-after when beautiful Bridget McCloud showed up on his ranch, cozying up to his little boy and kissing this single daddy till his soul caught on fire. Could this pretty city slicker be the bride this cowboy was looking for?

And look for Suzy Fenton's story, the exciting conclusion to this irresistible series, coming in late 1998, only from Silhouette Romance!

Available at your favorite retail outlet.

## *Silhouette* ROMANCE™

**HE CAN CHANGE A DIAPER IN THREE SECONDS FLAT BUT CHANGING HIS MIND ABOUT MARRIAGE MIGHT TAKE SOME DOING! HE'S ONE OF OUR**

**July 1998**
## ONE MAN'S PROMISE by Diana Whitney (SR#1307)
He promised to be the best dad possible for his daughter. Yet when successful architect Richard Matthews meets C. J. Moray, he wants to make another promise—this time to a wife.

**September 1998**
## THE COWBOY, THE BABY AND THE BRIDE-TO-BE by Cara Colter (SR#1319)
*Trouble,* thought Turner MacLeod when Shayla Morrison showed up at his ranch with his baby nephew in her arms. Could he take the chance of trusting his heart with this shy beauty?

**November 1998**
## ARE YOU MY DADDY? by Leanna Wilson (SR#1331)
She hated cowboys, but Marty Thomas was willing to do anything to help her son get his memory back—even pretend sexy cowboy Joe Rawlins was his father. Problem was, Joe thought he might like this to be a permanent position.

Available at your favorite retail outlet, only from

**♥ Silhouette ROMANCE™**

Look us up on-line at: http://www.romance.net          SRFFJ-N